"I tried to stay away," Ian said roughly. "But I can't, Michele."

She tried to push his hands off her, but somehow couldn't complete the motion; the moment she touched him, it was as if her own strength drained away. She was aching for his touch, and he wanted to move closer, to feel her in his arms again.

Michele's eyes closed suddenly and her slim hands gripped his wrists almost frantically. "I don't even trust you," she said in a voice that was nearly a moan. "Don't do this to me, Ian."

He drew a deep breath and grimly hung on to his control. How could they sort through the tangle of thoughts and emotions when the physical response to each other was this explosive? It was almost impossible to think at all. He'd never wanted a woman so badly in his life, and it was clear that her need was just as great.

"Michele, look at me," he ordered tautly.

She caught her breath, and her eyelids rose slowly to reveal haunted eyes the color of mountain fog.

"Let me teach you how to trust me. Give me a chance. Give us a chance, or we'll never know how good it can be be

# Star-Crossed
# LOVERS

## KAY HOOPER

BANTAM BOOKS
NEW YORK · TORONTO · LONDON · SYDNEY · AUCKLAND

STAR-CROSSED LOVERS
A Bantam FANFARE Book / March 1991

FANFARE and the portrayal of a boxed "ff" are trademarks of
Bantam Books, a division of Bantam Doubleday Dell
Publishing Group, Inc.

ISBN 0-553-28953-5

Published simultaneously in the United States and Canada

Bantam Books are published by Bantam Books, a division
of Bantam Doubleday Dell Publishing Group, Inc. Its trademark, consisting of the words "Bantam Books" and the
portrayal of a rooster, is Registered in U.S. Patent and
Trademark Office and in other countries. Marca Registrada.
Bantam Books, 666 Fifth Avenue, New York, New York 10103.

PRINTED IN THE UNITED STATES OF AMERICA

RAD    0  9  8  7  6  5  4  3  2  1

I will not let thee go.
The stars that crowd the summer skies
Have watched us so below
With all their million eyes,
I dare not let thee go

I will not let thee go.
I hold thee by too many bands:
Thou sayest farewell, and lo!
I have thee by the hands,
And will not let thee go.

—ROBERT BRIDGES

# Preface

No one knew how it had all started, or even when. A fascinated historian approached each family just after the turn of this century with the idea of researching and writing the story; each family shot at him. Aggrieved, he talked to the press instead, and a publisher had become interested enough to offer an advance.

With interest and support backing him up, the historian did a thorough job of research, and came up with a story colorful enough to satisfy all but himself. To the end of his days, he complained that he had never been able to find the source of the feud; he had traced a long and violent sequence of events all the way back to the fifteenth century, but even that didn't answer the basic question of when and how things went wrong.

Upon publication of his book, the historian was hardly surprised to learn that Cameron Stuart had promptly taken out an ad in a national newspaper proclaiming the feud had started, of course, with Tavis Logan throwing in with the house of York during the Wars of the Roses and then sealing his treachery with a marriage to a "weakly French slut."

Grady Logan, not to be outdone, had taken out a larger ad insisting it had been Wingate Stuart who had supported the York claim to the throne and then had stolen Tavis's French wife—unpardonable villainy. Which meant, Grady pointed out triumphantly, that Cameron was descended from that French slut.

And the feud went on.

The historian shook his head and sighed while newspapers and magazines ran bits of his book to feed curious readers.

It had been a Logan, said the Stuarts, who had whispered gently but forcefully into Henry VIII's ear to rid himself of his Spanish queen, thus helping to oust Catherine of Aragon. A Stuart, cried the Logans, had rigged the evidence that had lost Anne Boleyn her head.

Jane Seymour, having died in childbirth, apparently escaped the effects of the Stuart-Logan feud, but popular belief held that Anne of Cleves was accepted by Henry only because of the flattering portrait a Logan had put before him; a Stuart had gleefully helped Henry out of that marriage.

Logan retaliated by subtly pointing out the prettiness of Catherine Howard at court, and Stuart caused her downfall—and the loss of her head—by guiding the king's council to find strong evidence of her infidelity. Both sides claimed the happy marriage Henry enjoyed with Catherine Parr.

It seemed there was much fodder for the feud during Henry's reign, between the king's marriages and his strong mistrust of the Plantagenets, to say nothing of his break with Rome. Since both Logan and Stuart were of the old nobility, it seemed to have been the height of insanity to cut at each other by using a suspicious king as a tool—but both, somehow, survived.

They survived also the short reign of the last Tudor king, Edward VI, the nine-days' "reign" of Lady Jane Grey, and the few years of "Bloody" Mary I. Both Logan and Stuart were somewhat foolhardy when it came to their feud, but neither was fool enough to use Elizabeth I as they had her father, Henry; nor were they reckless enough to encourage handsome sons to chase after the Virgin Queen.

Both Stuart and Logan had eyed askance Elizabeth's successor James I, winced when James's son Charles I declared war on Spain, and shook their heads when he lost his. They had kept quiet and still while Cromwell "reigned" and were relieved when Charles II was crowned.

By the time George III began having his troubles with madness, both Logan and Stuart, separately, of course, had decided to try their luck with America. And both were incredibly lucky in their adopted land; but the family feud went on.

Too late to choose opposite sides in the Revolution, they lost no opportunity in later years and generations to keep feeding the fire. (They had a fine time during the Civil War, for example, though hampered a mite by the fact that both families lived in the Deep South.) What one supported, the other attempted to destroy; what one had, the other had to better.

At times the feud was ridiculous, such as when Jeb Logan painted his privy red to match Cal Stuart's house. Cal had retaliated by creeping over one night to move the privy behind its pit; when Jeb came out for his before-bed visit and walked into the pit, his enraged screams could be heard for miles.

And, inevitably, the feud was sometimes tragic. Stuarts and Logans had been killing each other, for good and bad reasons—or no reason at all—for generations, and the move to America did not stop that. Theirs was a long list of duels, brawls, and deaths. They stole property from one another, destroyed property, sabotaged each other's reputations and business dealings. They imbued their children with their hatred, encouraging more destruction and revenge for destruction.

The historian had discovered a single pattern in the feud which he found fascinating, but no one else seemed to grasp its significance. As nearly as he could determine from the historical evidence, it appeared that in each generation events conspired to produce a critical moment during which the feud could have been stopped.

It seemed to happen in the youth of each generation, when they themselves had no personal grievance against each other and might have risen above the hatred of their elders. But, inevitably, the critical moment was overlooked, or discounted, or those involved simply failed to pass the test. They were drawn into the feud and found their own reasons for continuing it. None had been able to find within themselves whatever was needed to stop the hate.

On it went, a circle with no beginning and no foreseeable ending. In sheer pigheaded spite they chose similar homes, similar businesses, and similar lives. Flying in the face of all logic, they chose to live near one another, so that children brought up to hate were pointed at specific targets.

Long after other well-known family feuds had ended, wounds healed and forgotten, the Stuarts and Logans continued to hate and plot, until the situation was ripe for a shocking conclusion.

It was a pity the historian couldn't have lived to see the finale. He would have loved it.

# Prologue

"Damn him!" Charles Logan looked at his son with bitter gray eyes. "I don't suppose we can prove it?"

Jonathan Logan shook his head, the same hard emotion reflected in his blue eyes. "Not a chance, Dad. The inspector was smart enough not to put the money in his own bank account, and my source at city hall won't go on the record with what he knows."

"But he's sure it was Stuart?"

"Who else?" Jonathan laughed shortly. "The inspector was paid to keep us tied up for weeks while he looks at every piece of wire in the building; he's not about to accept our word that the electrical work is up to code. And you can bet Stuart's building has already been approved. Unless we do something to slow Stuart down, we don't have a hope in hell."

The elder Logan turned to stare out the window of his tenth-floor office. In the distance, between two other buildings, he could see his own latest effort rearing skyward. From the outside it looked complete, but even now his crews were at work doing what they could inside it. Until the inspector passed all the wiring in the massive building, most of the work couldn't be finished.

Though always fiercely competitive with his nemesis, Charles Logan never permitted slipshod work due to haste. But on this job, he had pushed his crews to do it right and *fast*, because there was so much at stake.

And now . . .

"Dad? We aren't going to take this lying down?" Jonathan's voice was incredulous. "If Stuart finishes his building first, he'll get the Techtron contract and it's worth millions. He'll crow all over Atlanta that he beat us—"

"He's not going to beat us." Charles's voice was deadly quiet. "No matter what we have to do, he's not going to beat us."

Frowning, Brandon Stuart gazed out his office window as he listened to one of his foremen. He said nothing until the man finished his report, then turned to stare at the man.

"We've dealt with these suppliers for years, Carl. What the hell's going on?"

The foreman shrugged helplessly. "Beats me, boss. To hear them tell it, half the material we order is out of stock, and the other half turns out to be not what we ordered. I've had to send four trucks back just this morning. It feels to me like we're being stonewalled."

"Logan," Brandon Stuart said, making the name a curse.

The foreman blinked. "I don't see how, boss. Unless—well, I suppose they could be favoring his orders over ours. All the places we're having trouble with supply him too."

"I want it stopped," Stuart said in a voice that grated. "I don't care what it takes, or what it costs, I want it stopped. I won't let that bastard beat me!"


"They don't know about it?"

"No, my love, they don't. They don't know how strongly the seeds of hate took root."

Troubled, she said, "Dangerous."

Cyrus Fortune smiled at his lady, but though the smile glowed with the love he always showed her, there was little reassurance in it. "The wild card, I'm afraid. I can't be sure how the others will react to it. But a festering wound must be opened to let the poison out."

"She'll be hurt."

Cyrus sighed heavily, his benign dark eyes fully expressing his sorrow. "I don't see how it can be avoided. That wasn't a part of my plan. But I should have anticipated what he would do."

"Nonsense." Her tone was bracing, but she softened it with a smile. "At any rate, I feel sure you'll do what you can to lessen any unanticipated blows."

"What I can." Cyrus glanced out the small window at the thick white clouds beneath them and sighed again. "But where there is love—real or manufactured—there must be pain as well. Some blows can't be softened."

There was nothing she could say to that, and

she knew him too well to pretend answers she didn't have. Instead, her small hand slipped into his, and she remained silent while the sleek jet cut downward through the clouds toward its landing on the island of Martinique.

# One

"You need help?"

They faced each other, surprise in both their expressions instantly supplanted by mistrust and wariness. He stopped dead in his tracks as though he'd run into a wall, and she felt a sudden compulsion to pick up something heavy.

Michele Logan recovered first, throwing off impulses that were ridiculous, she told herself. "Damn thing died on me," she said, waving a hand at the rental compact parked off the side of the road. She looked at her would-be rescuer and swallowed a giggle—surprising herself at the burst of humor and wondering if chivalry was dead, choked to death long ago by the Logans and the Stuarts.

"I'll look at it," he offered, proving that Stuarts could overcome destructive impulses just as well as Logans.

At least when the familiar battleground was more than two thousand miles away.

Michele stood back, still conscious of her own wary tension, and watched Ian Stuart bend down to peer beneath the car's raised hood. She caught herself glancing up and down the deserted road, and felt like laughing aloud to discover she was fearful of even being seen with a Stuart.

Her father, an otherwise reasonable man, would have been tempted to disinherit her after one glance at her companion . . . or thunder about doing so.

But her father was back in Atlanta, not here on the island paradise of Martinique. In fact, there was no one here who could possibly know or care that representatives from both sides of a very old feud had unexpectedly encountered each other on the road to Fort-de-France.

She studied the enemy, trying to be as objective as possible. He was a big man, with powerful shoulders setting off an obviously athletic body of unusual strength. He was the kind of man who looked sexy in jeans and formal clothing alike, drawing feminine stares wherever he went. At the present, he was wearing jeans and a pullover shirt. He had wheat-gold hair worn thick and just shaggy enough to make a woman want to run her fingers through the shining strands.

*Most women,* Michele reminded herself, surprised that she had to. *But not me.*

She also reminded herself that she had never been attracted to fair men, but then had to admit silently that blond hair went awfully well with a tanned, handsome face and ice-blue eyes. Still, Ian Stuart was the last man in the world she could ever be drawn to.

In a peculiar way, they knew each other well. Ian Stuart and Michele's brother, Jonathan, were the same age, and the families both owned houses and businesses in Atlanta, Georgia. As children, Michele and Jon had competed against Ian in horse shows and rodeos, and the boys had brawled on and off their different schools' football fields.

Michele knew for a fact that Jon had lost at least one high-school girlfriend to Ian Stuart, and that Ian had lost two desired horses at auction to Jon's determined bidding.

Michele was twenty-six, Ian was thirty-one, and this was the first time in their adult lives that they had met face to face and alone.

She didn't know how to react to the unexpected situation. All her life she had listened to invectives directed at the Stuarts in general and their neighbors in particular; she'd even spat a few curses of her own. She could have listed their treacheries going all the way back to the fifteenth century. Instinct told her she should be raining invectives of her own now, but common sense questioned the need for it.

Ian looked up and saw her watching him, his pale blue eyes as wary as her own probably were. He straightened slowly and looked at her for a moment in silence, then glanced at the compact. "This needs a mechanic, which I'm not," he said in a neutral tone. "I'm going into Fort-de-France; I can send a tow truck back. Or," he added after a moment, "I can give you a lift."

Michele found herself wondering if the earth would open up and swallow them both at this heresy, and laughed as she realized her muscles were braced for a thunderclap. It was ridiculous! "Thanks, I'd appreciate a lift," she said. "I can call the rental company from the hotel and have them deal with it."

"Where are you staying?"

"The Arcadia."

"So am I."

Moments later, sitting comfortably beside Ian in his own rental car, she dismissed the fleeting guilt at her traitorous behavior. Because it *wasn't* traitorous, not really. She was a sensible woman and saw no reason why she should prefer to roast in the hot sun rather than accept a brief ride from a man who had never done her an injury.

"Lucky you came along," she ventured casually. "I might have been stuck out here all day." There had been a few passing cars, but none had stopped.

"I half expected you to throw the offer of a ride back in my face," he murmured.

"At home, I might have," she admitted, turning her head to gaze at the colorful tropical landscape all around them. "But who can fight in paradise?"

Ian sent her a glance, taking the opportunity of her distraction to study her unobtrusively. It had been years since he'd been this close to Michele Logan. On that last memorable occasion, she'd been thrown by her horse during warm-ups for a Grand Prix jumping event, and he had offered her a hand up. Sixteen-year-old Michele had rewarded him for his pains by roundly cursing him, and had regained her feet under her own power.

She had also beaten him in the event.

Ten years had changed her . . . a lot. Then she'd been thin as a rail and all legs; she was slender now, but no one would ever compare her to a rail. The faded jeans and pale blue T-shirt she wore clung to every curve, and those curves were voluptuous enough to inspire erotic fantasies. Her legs were still long, but they, too, were the stuff of men's dreams. Her waist-length black hair, wild as a colt's mane for most of her childhood, was confined neatly in a French braid now, and the severe style emphasized the delicate bone structure of her lovely face. Those bones had seemed awkwardly arranged during her childhood and adolescence, but maturity had smoothed sharp planes and angles into striking beauty.

On the rare occasions in the past when Ian had seen her—at a distance, naturally, and usually across crowded rooms—he had always been conscious of faint surprise. From tall, robust parents of average looks had come this slight, smoke-eyed, raven-haired woman of unusual and distinctive beauty; she was a throwback to the Celtic ancestors she and Ian could both claim, as physically unlike her present-day family as he was unlike his own.

Ian wondered if the differences were only physical; her brother Jon would have chosen a ride with the devil over one with a Stuart.

Feeling her attention shift back to him, he said, "What are you doing in paradise?"

"Vacationing," she answered in the same pleasant tone she'd been using, her low voice rather husky. "November in Atlanta was unbearable. All that cold rain. I had vacation time coming to me, and the company wasn't willing to let me take it next year. So, Martinique."

She had chosen not to enter the family construction business, he knew. He thought it odd, but interesting that she was employed by a large insurance company as an investigator.

"I'd planned to come with a friend," Michele

said, "but she got held up by her job and won't be arriving for a few more days. How about you?"

"Business," he answered. "I'm supposed to be meeting a potential client here, but he's been delayed."

"You're an architect, aren't you?"

He nodded, very conscious that she was looking intently at him. His awareness of her surprised him more than a little. "Like your brother," he said, and from the corner of his eye saw her grimace slightly.

"I wonder if, pardon the pun, that was by design."

Smiling faintly, he said, "Jon and I both being architects? I don't know about your father, but mine wasn't happy with my career choice. He felt growing up around the construction business provided all the knowledge I'd need to take over the company one day. I was born to follow plans, he said, not draw them."

She laughed softly, and he was astonished to realize how focused his senses were on her. It was just like the first instant he'd recognized her there by the car, when he had felt the shocked wariness of encountering not an enemy, but something totally unexpected.

"Not by design then," she said dryly. "Dad hit the roof when Jon announced his career plans. He complained that all those summers working for the firm had been wasted. He's come around in the last few years, though, especially after Jon convinced him that an architect would be an asset to the family business."

"Mine still has reservations," Ian said. "We argue about once a month, regular as clockwork."

"Who wins?" she asked, amused.

"Me. Dad says he takes consolation in the knowledge that strong-minded men breed strong-minded sons."

"And daughters," Michele commented somewhat dryly.

"Your father didn't like your being an investigator?"

If she was surprised by his knowledge, it didn't show on her face. "Are you kidding? Whenever he catches my eye, Dad looks wistfully at some of the old paintings hanging on the walls of our house. All done by our ancestral Southern belles, of course. He didn't mind my showing horses or running barrels in the rodeo, but he winces whenever he has to face the fact that his gently nurtured daughter is a licensed investigator."

"Were you never tempted to get into the family business?"

Michele was silent for a moment, her gaze directed at the windshield but unfocused. Then she looked at Ian. "The business end of it interested me, but some of Dad's goals weren't mine. I couldn't see expending so much energy in a rivalry that was so . . . bitter."

It was the first time either of them had mentioned the feud. Ian wanted to probe her feelings on the matter, especially since her statements indicated she was far less rabid about it than her father and brother. But they reached the hotel just then, and as he pulled the car into the circular entrance drive, he felt a definite reluctance to part company with Michele Logan.

A parking valet came out to take the car, and they walked into the cool lobby together, both silent. Neither spoke until they were in the elevator. Michele pushed the button for her floor, watched him follow suit, and realized absently that his room was three floors above hers. Then Ian broke the silence in a mild tone.

"We're both alone here for the time being. Have dinner with me tonight."

Michele was conscious of shock, but it took her several seconds to realize why.

Because he was a Stuart.

All her life, she had been told repeatedly and with passionate insistence that there was nothing on earth worse than a Stuart—except two of them. Told, moreover, by the father she had always adored. And no matter what logical protests her rational mind could counter with, it was impossible for her to discount what had been drummed into her since childhood.

As the elevator doors opened onto her floor, Ian pressed a button on the control panel to hold them open. He looked at her steadily. "Here at the hotel, of course. The food's great."

She drew a short breath, freed at last from a cold place she was horrified to find inside her. A place that had been sown with dark seeds. She felt shaken and was aware of an almost overpowering relief; the seeds might have been sown, but there was nothing dark and twisted growing there. Only an echo of what might have been.

Or what might yet be.

That flashing insight reminded her that she was far more than a mere continuation of a story that had been written in stone five hundred years ago. She was an individual with her own thoughts and beliefs, and it was entirely up to her whether she *chose* to hate another person—with or without sufficient cause.

And neither this man nor his family had given her any cause to hate.

"Michele?"

Had he ever said her name? She didn't think so. It felt unfamiliar coming from him, a roughly beautiful sound like nothing she'd ever heard before. She looked up at him, uncertain and more than a little wary, but the cool hint of challenge in his eyes made her decide. "Sure." Her voice was unsteady, and she concentrated on firming it up. "I'd be glad of the company."

Ian smiled. "Good. I'll meet you in the lobby, then. Around seven?"

Michele nodded. "I'll be there. And thanks for the rescue, Ian."

"Anytime."

She got off the elevator, almost immediately turning right to head down the hallway to her room. It wasn't until she was inside that a shaken laugh escaped her. She felt strange, as if all her emotions had been tumbled about and left in a heap.

She dropped her purse on the big bed and kicked off her sandals, then went to adjust the temperature of the air conditioning. It was unsettling to discover the room was actually cool according to the thermostat; it seemed hot to her. Deciding firmly that the time spent in the sun after her car broke down had given her a very mild case of heat exhaustion, she called room service for a pitcher of iced tea. She spent the next few minutes on the phone with the car rental company, then changed into shorts and went to let the waiter in with her order.

After he'd gone, she banked the pillows on her bed and curled up with a glass of cold tea. She'd turned the television on to a news channel, but didn't pay much attention even though she stared at the screen.

Ian Stuart. A peripheral part of her life for nearly as long as she could remember, he had suddenly appeared center stage with no warning. And she didn't know how she felt about that.

A scene from ten years before sprang vividly into her mind, surprising her with its clarity. A show ring during warm-ups for a Grand Prix event. She'd been riding a young horse, expecting nothing from him and intending only to school him over moderate jumps so he could become accustomed to shows. He had balked at the third jump and shied violently, throwing her.

Ian had been there, riding an experienced jumper, and he had been the first to offer her a hand up. Mortified at having been dumped like a Sunday rider practically at his feet, she had spat a few biting comments on his ancestry and had picked herself up without his help. The sting to her pride had been painful, and it was lucky her young horse wasn't a timid one who would have been easily ruined by being pushed too hard too soon; when she rode him into the ring later, she was riding fiercely to win.

She had held her mount with iron control, refusing to let him run out at the jumps, driving him over them with sheer determination, riding him harder than ever before. The result had been a spectacular victory, and her horse had become the best jumper she'd ever owned.

All because of embarrassment.

The memory gave her pause. Was it only the ten years between sixteen and twenty-six that made her feel differently about Ian Stuart now? Or *did* she feel differently? She hadn't ridden to beat him that day because of family rivalry; the feud between their fathers hadn't even entered her head. She had done it because the toss had made her feel like a fool, and she'd wanted to show Ian that she was a first-rate rider and could handle any horse.

Childish pride, she decided. That was all. She hadn't even thought about Ian during the years after that occasion. Oh, she'd seen him from time to time at a distance at social or charity events, and both her father and Jon had offered frequent scathing remarks about the doings of Ian and his father. But she hadn't thought about him consciously, hadn't considered his unique and disturbing place in her life. She'd been busy finishing school, going to college, getting a job. She had dated regularly, but hadn't become deeply involved with any of the men she saw.

The phone on the nightstand rang, and Michele nearly jumped out of her skin. Grimacing, she picked up the receiver. "Hello?"

"They've done it to us again," Jon announced without preamble.

She didn't have to ask who "they" were, or why her brother had called to tell her about it; Jon tended to keep in touch with her almost daily if she was away from home, and was always quick to report the latest underhanded dealings by the Stuarts.

"What now?" she asked, suppressing the knowledge that her brother would demand her immediate return if she told him that Ian was in Martinique and in the same hotel.

"They've bribed half the inspectors, that's what." As always, when he spoke of the Stuarts his normally pleasant voice was hard. "Our crews are sitting on their duffs waiting for the final inspections of the electrical and plumbing work, and the inspectors are staring at every piece of wire and pipe in the damned building."

"Jon, you don't really believe they've bribed city officials?" She made the attempt even though she knew it would be fruitless.

"Payoffs and kickbacks. Hell, you know how it works."

"I don't suppose you have any proof?"

"Michele, what's wrong with you? Since when have the Stuarts been stupid enough to leave fingerprints?" Even that backhanded compliment was grudging.

She leaned back against the headboard of the bed and sighed softly. She loved her brother, but, like their father, he had a wide blind spot when it came to the Stuarts. "Sorry," she said in a light tone. "I guess it's just hard to hate in paradise."

Jon grunted a response that could have meant anything, then asked, "Is Jackie with you?"

"No, she was delayed. She'll be here in a few days."

"What're you going to do?"

Michele could hardly help but laugh. "Brother dear, I believe I can entertain myself for a few days alone. I've been pretty good at that since I left the crib."

"Well, be careful." He sounded amused by her tart reply, but also a bit restless. "Big girls have more to worry about than little ones, and you're a long way from home."

"I'll be fine, Jon. You just promise me that you and Dad won't try some harebrained stunt to get even with the Stuarts for what you *think* they're doing."

He laughed. "I'll probably talk to you tomorrow, Misha."

His childhood nickname for her reassured her only a little, because he hadn't promised. "Jon—"

"Don't fall for some tall, dark stranger. Bye."

Michele cradled the receiver, troubled. She got up to refill her glass, then settled back on the bed. She didn't feel guilty at not having told Jon about Ian's presence. Her brother had always been overly protective of her when it came to men, and he would have reacted violently to the knowledge.

But she was disturbed, both by what could be happening in Atlanta and by her own actions here. Her rational mind told her that having dinner with a man in the hotel was nothing to be worried about, but the fact that the man was Ian Stuart troubled her a great deal.

She glanced at the clock on the nightstand. Five. In two hours, she was supposed to sit down to a civilized meal with the sworn enemy of her father and brother. The very thought seemed melodramatic, but Michele wasn't tempted to laugh, or even to mock it. She was only too aware that the simple act of having dinner with Ian Stuart was enough to tear violently the fabric of her family.

If they ever found out.


He was standing near the desk in the lobby when Michele came out of the elevator, and she walked toward him steadily with the unnerved feeling of having burned her bridges. She had dressed to give herself courage; the midnight-blue linen dress she wore was full-skirted and high-necked, but left her back and arms bare, and she knew the style suited her.

He must have thought so, too, for she could see the appreciation in his striking pale blue eyes as he looked at her. He, too, was dressed informally in a light-brown jacket and dark slacks, with his white shirt open at the throat.

"I thought you might stand me up," he murmured as she reached him.

"I almost did," she admitted honestly.

"What made you change your mind?"

Michele drew a short breath. "Sheer cussedness, I guess. I like to make up my own mind about things."

"And people?"

"And people." She managed a smile.

Ian smiled slightly as well, but his eyes were very intent. "Of course, the fact that no one's going to know about this didn't influence you at all."

"Of course not. Besides, you could have hired a photographer to take pictures to send to my father." She blinked, conscious of shock at her own words.

Ian took her arm lightly and began leading her across the lobby toward the dining room. "I didn't."

"I'm sorry. I don't know why I said that."

"Because you've been taught to suspect the motives of anyone named Stuart."

"Do you suspect my motives?"

"No."

Michele looked up at him as they walked, a little surprised to find that her head barely topped his shoulder even though she was wearing heels. "Why not?" She was honestly curious, wondering if their upbringings had been so different or if Ian had simply risen above his.

Ian didn't answer until they'd been shown to their table in the quiet restaurant. When they were supplied with menus and left alone again, he looked across the table at her. "Because I think you're honest, Michele. If you wanted to fight me, you'd do it openly."

"With all my motives flying like flags?"

"Yes. I wish you could believe the same about me."

She hesitated, but couldn't lie. "I want to. The rational part of me does."

"But," he murmured.

Michele nodded. "But. I was thinking about it up in my room. Do you suppose that after five hundred years it's become imbedded in the genes?"

"I'd hate to believe that."

"So would I." She bent her head and began studying the menu, adding lightly, "I'm starved. I skipped lunch so I could explore the island."

The soft lighting in the dining room combined with her black hair and gleaming blue dress to lend her a curiously insubstantial air. And her manner toward him intensified the impression, because she was troubled and wary. Ian couldn't stop looking at her, even as he told himself this was worse than reckless, it was insane.

He wasn't worried about sitting across a dinner table from Michele Logan; that was certainly harmless and even his father—after an initial explosion—would be able to make little of it. What bothered him was his reaction to her. Every fleeting expression in her smoke-gray eyes fascinated him, and her delicate face held his gaze as if she were his lodestar.

When he had taken her arm and walked beside her through the lobby, he had been vividly aware of her warmth, of the faintly spicy scent of her perfume. He had wanted to put his hand on her bare back, to touch the pale gold skin that looked so soft and silky. Then she had glanced up at him with those haunting eyes, and he'd felt a jolt to some part of him. He didn't know what it meant, but he knew instinctively that something had been forever changed by it.

"I think I'll have the chicken." She looked at him, faint color rising in her cheeks. "How about you?"

He realized that she had felt him staring at her, that she was disturbed by the steady gaze. "The same," he said, without the faintest idea of what he was agreeing to.

Michele folded her hands over the menu and fixed her eyes on them. In a conversational tone, she said, "What we were talking about before is something neither of us can forget, you know. Suspicions. Whether they're imbedded in the genes or the mind, they're still there."

"I don't have any reason to hate you, Michele. And you have no reason to hate me."

She nodded. "I know. But not hating is one thing; becoming friends is something else. Even if we could, I mean. Even if we wanted to. Because it isn't just us."

"Why?" He leaned toward her unconsciously, wanting her to look at him so he could see what she was thinking and feeling. He didn't think about what he was saying, he simply felt compelled to make her understand something that was very clear to him. "It's just us here, Michele. No fathers or brothers looking over our shoulders. Nobody around who gives a damn if we're enemies, friends . . . or lovers."

She felt a strange flare of heat at the last word and didn't know if it was the word itself or the husky way he said it that caused her reaction. She didn't dare meet his eyes because she was half afraid of what she might find in his gaze. Tension wound tightly inside her, like a spring coiling, and she couldn't seem to hold her breathing steady.

"Michele?"

Softly, still without looking at him, she said, "When I was a little girl, I didn't know that Stuart was a name. I'd heard my father say it many times, but all I knew from his tone of voice was that a 'Stuart' was something bad."

Very deliberately, he reached across the table and covered her folded hands with one of his own. "I thought Logan was a curse until I was seven. But I'm not seven anymore. And you're not a little girl. We have to start with just us, Michele. Or else blindly follow twenty generations of tradition in our families."

She stared at the big hand covering hers, feeling the warmth and heavy strength of it. Finally, she raised her eyes to his, seeing in them some of the intensity that she had felt earlier. "I don't think I'd be a very good trailblazer," she said unsteadily. "There's so much I'd be risking. So much I could lose. Would lose." Her father's love. Her brother's.

For a brief moment, Ian's hand tightened over hers, then he leaned back and withdrew from her. "All right," he said quietly. "I suppose that not hating is something."

Ian signaled the waiter, going on in the same mild tone. "We can at least have dinner in peace; the families don't have to know we're even on the same island."

Michele gave her order and listened as he gave his. She felt a strong sense of loss and also a bitter feeling of failure. She had never really failed in her life, not at anything that mattered to her—and somehow Ian mattered to her very much. She wasn't sure why, perhaps simply because it *was* her nature to make up her own mind about things. Sometimes, there was no choice to make. If she could have believed that the feud could be stopped because she and Ian made peace between them, she would have risked it, she told herself fiercely. But she knew both her father and brother too well to think that was possible.

"Don't look so troubled," Ian said softly. "Maybe when it's our turn to carry the torch, we can do a better job with it."

"No," she said. "Maybe you don't want to hate, but Jon does. Dad's poisoned him. He's heard so much more than I have. I don't know, maybe he got the brunt of it because he was older. Or maybe because he'd always keep the Logan name. Dad isn't rational where you're concerned. And no matter how good your intentions are, Ian, if somebody hates you long enough and tries to hurt you often enough, you'll hate too."

Ian frowned slightly. "It sounds as if your father is more bitter than mine. Do you know why?"

She shook her head. "No. But Jon knows something. When we were younger he said that your father had done something terrible to ours a long time ago. He wouldn't tell me what it was."

"It must have had something to do with a woman."

She was surprised. "Why do you say that?"

"Otherwise, Jon would have told you."

Michele thought about that, and somewhere deep inside she felt a little chill. Had some unknown woman intensified an already bitter rivalry? What had happened? Women were vulnerable when men feuded; they could be hurt in so many ways. They could be used as weapon or as victim. As soon as that thought occurred to her, she felt another chill and then anger hard on the heels of it. These damned *suspicions*! Ian had merely suggested that the two of them make peace, not crawl into bed together.

Into bed . . . together . . .

Her breathing seemed to stop for an instant, and a wave of dizziness swept over her. Images flashed in her mind, images that were raw and powerful— and undeniably exciting. For the first time in her life, she felt the shocked awareness of her own sexuality, and the images were so strong they were almost overpowering. The thought of being in bed with Ian Stuart triggered a surge of emotions as confused as they were complex.

"What are you thinking?" he asked suddenly.

Michele felt heat rise in her face. She wasn't about to confess the erotic images still playing through her mind, not the least because they shocked her to her bones. "I was . . . wishing that it was simple. Wishing it was just us." She heard the husky words emerge, and felt another jolt because she knew it was true.

"Would you trust me then?"

"I don't know. But I'd only be risking myself if I took the chance."

The waiter arrived and began to serve their food just then, and Ian didn't respond to what she'd said.

Michele was grateful for the reprieve, using it to try desperately to cope with these stunning, unexpected, and wholly unfamiliar feelings. She ate food she didn't taste, bewildered by what had happened to her—and why it had happened.

Why *had* it happened? Why had her chance encounter with Ian and the reckless act of having dinner with him sparked these wild surges of desire? How could she possibly feel such things for this man of all men? She had never felt desire until now, not at all; her strongest interest in a man had been mild and detached compared to this.

But now . . .

Tension coiled in her as her emotions churned chaotically. Make peace with Ian? No, that would never be possible now. Even if it were just the two of them, she knew that what she wanted of him had little to do with peace. It was as if some barrier inside her had collapsed into rubble at the slightest touch, and what she saw beyond that shattered wall terrified her.

"Michele?"

She looked up at him, seeing a lean, handsome face that was all too dreadfully familiar now, because something, some deeply buried instinct, told her it had always been behind that wall. Waiting.

It was too much to accept, to think about; she had to get away from it. She set her fork aside automatically and pushed her chair back. "Excuse me," she murmured, rising jerkily to her feet.

"Michele, what's wrong?" He was on his feet as well, staring at her with concern and something else in his eyes.

She couldn't answer him, because all the answers were so terribly dangerous. Without another word, she hurried away from their table. She heard him call after her, but the sound of her name only made her move faster. She was almost running by the time she reached the lobby, and barely noticed a few startled faces as she raced across and fled out into the night.

The hotel boasted a strip of private beach, deserted this late, and it was there Michele ran. She kicked off her heels almost as soon as she left the hotel, leaving them where they fell. She passed the blue-lit pool and blindly followed the path through the lush garden until she felt sand under her feet and saw the moonlit darkness of the ocean.

When she reached the water she turned, racing on the wet sand. For years she'd made a habit of morning runs to keep in shape. She ran fast now, the wind tearing her hair free of its braid and whipping her skirt out behind her. She ran because she had to escape.

# Two

"Michele!"

He caught up with her at the northwest end of the beach as she approached a ridge of volcanic rock jutting up from the sand that marked the boundary of the hotel's private beach.

When he grabbed her hand and forced her to stop, pulling her around to face him, she felt an instant of anger and half raised her free hand as if she would have pounded on his broad chest.

She stared up at him, her clenched hand motionless now. She could see him clearly in the moonlight, and she wished it was dark because she knew he could see her just as clearly.

"What are you running from?" he demanded.

Almost idly, she noted that he was in excellent shape since he wasn't even breathing hard from the race. Her own heart was pounding, and she couldn't seem to draw enough air into her lungs. "Let me go," she demanded.

He released her hand but only so that he could grasp both her shoulders firmly. "I want to know why you're running, Michele."

She felt smothered by him, trapped, despite the open space all around them. He was so big, and he'd caught her all too easily and quickly in spite of her head start. She couldn't escape him. But she had to stop this before something irrevocable happened, before it was too late. Panic rose in her, and this time her fists did pound against his chest.

"Let me go! I won't let you do this to me, I won't!"

Ian barely felt the blows. He had run after her instinctively, thinking only of stopping her because there had been something wild and frightened in her eyes. It was in her voice now, in the supple strength of her slender body as she fought desperately to get away from him. Her words made no sense to him, but the thin sound of her voice did. She was afraid of him somehow, almost terrified, and the realization was like a knife in his chest.

He should have released her simply to reassure her that he wouldn't hurt her, but he didn't want to see her run away from him again. Without stopping to think, he pulled her into his arms, trapping her hands between them and holding her firmly.

"Michele, stop it. Be still. I'm not going to hurt you." He forced himself to speak quietly. She went on struggling for a moment, but then her breath caught as her movements made her lower body press against his, and she seemed to freeze.

A small wave lapped over their feet gently. His

hands were on her bare back now, and her skin was every bit as soft and smooth as it looked. Her hair had come loose, tumbling down her back and over his hands like warm, heavy silk. She was utterly still, hardly seeming to breathe, but her delicate body was pressed against his and he could feel every curve, feel the warmth of her.

"No," she said in a very soft but distinct voice. Her head tilted back slowly as she looked up at him, and moonlight shimmered darkly in her eyes. Against his chest, her fingers uncurled and spread, but she didn't try to push him away.

His own fingers were moving, lightly probing the straightness of her spine as one hand slid up toward her nape and the other found the small of her back. She felt so fragile against him, so feminine, and his entire body was reacting wildly, all his senses so sharpened it was almost painful. His heart hammered against his ribs, and a jolt of pure, raw desire settled in his loins with a throbbing ache.

"No?" he murmured, knowing that they weren't talking about fear now. Her eyes were wide, fixed on his face, her lips slightly parted and trembling.

"Don't do this. Don't let this happen." Her voice was little more than a whisper.

His arms tightened around her. "You knew it would happen, didn't you? That's why you ran."

The admission she had made horrified her, leaving her painfully vulnerable. "That's insane! How could I possibly even think— Let me go, Ian!"

"You knew," he repeated, his voice deepening and going rough. "You felt it too."

Michele shook her head, but it was a helpless not a negative gesture. If she had felt trapped before, it was nothing compared to this feeling. The

very suddenness and stark force of the attraction
had granted her no time to find a defense, and her
effort to escape had been useless. And somewhere
inside her, deeper than thought, was an acknowl-
edgment of inevitability.

Being in his arms felt so *right*. Her body had
known that the instant it had touched his, and she
couldn't deny the sharp excitement surging through
her.

Michele felt him move, a subtle shifting that
brought her more intimately against him. She gasped
at the sensation and managed a single, strangled
protest. "Don't."

Ian bent his head slowly, blocking out the moonlight until all she could see was the glimmer of his
eyes. Her own eyes closed slowly as his lips touched
hers. For an instant she sensed that she was poised
on the brink, as if she still had a choice. But then
the choice was made, and there was no going back.
She felt herself melt even closer against him, her
arms lifting to his neck, her mouth opening wildly
beneath the increasing pressure of his.

As easily and simply as that, something detonated between them, and the shock waves of it made
them both shudder. Ian gathered her even closer,
lifting her up against him so that she was nearly off
her feet. Her breasts were pressed to his chest, burning him even through their clothing, and her yielding loins fit his as if their bodies had been made for
each other.

Michele was drowning in waves of heat, totally
helpless against what was happening. She had been
kissed before, but the experience had always left her
unmoved. Apparently she wasn't a sensual woman;
she had never felt the slightest urge to go beyond

kisses. In Ian's arms, though, no simple urge drove her; the need to be closer, to have more of him, was a compulsion stronger than anything she'd ever felt before.

His mouth was hard and hungry, the deep exploration of his tongue making her entire body quiver. She responded without thought or hesitation, the urgency inside her sweeping all else before it in a tide of need. Every stark, new sensation was somehow familiar, as if she had always known how it would be with him. The hard strength of his chest compressing her aching breasts, his taut belly against hers, the throbbing fullness of his loins nestled intimately in her yielding softness—it was all familiar and what her body craved.

His hand tangled in her hair, and his legs widened as his other hand slid below the small of her back to hold her harder against him. Pleasure exploded inside her, hot and dizzying, and a moan of desire caught raggedly in her throat. Then he lifted his head abruptly, and the sound she made in response was a murmur of disappointment.

"Michele." His voice was dark, liquid, the heavy need in it a sound that was almost pain. His entire body was taut, and his chest rose and fell as if he had run some desperate race.

"Don't stop," she whispered, tightening her arms around his neck as she tried to pull his head back down.

For an instant, Ian almost gave in. The slender body in his arms was warm and willing, moving against him even now with a need that matched his own. And her breathy plea snatched at his control, the implicit surrender filling his mind until he could hardly think of anything but drawing her down to the wet sand and fusing their bodies together in a heated mating. Only the sure knowledge that she would hate him afterward gave him the will to stop.

Both his hands found her hips, and he gently forced her lower body away from his. She squirmed in his hold, trying to move closer again, and Ian bit back a groan. Harshly, he demanded, "Who am I, Michele?"

She blinked up at him, bewildered. "Ian," she murmured.

His hands tightened, and he made himself go on, hating this. "Ian what? Finish it."

Her lips, pouty from his kisses, quivered suddenly, and she went still in his grasp. "Stuart," she whispered.

"Is that who you want in your bed?"

The stark question went through Michele like a cold knife, bringing sanity at last. Her arms were still around his neck. She removed them slowly, then stepped jerkily back until his hands dropped from her. Her legs were shaking, her body was shaking, and it hurt to breathe. Part of her wanted to cry out to him in anguish, demanding to know why he had spoiled it, why he'd had to remind her of what they were; another part of her was trying to cope with the enormity of what she'd almost done.

"Thanks . . . for reminding me," she forced herself to say as steadily as possible.

"I want you, Michele," he said in a low voice that was almost guttural. "Right now, right here in the sand, I want you."

She was dimly aware of understanding that he had stopped because the choice she would have made in the heat of desire was a blind one.

Michele knew it too. Her mind had been programmed implacably against him for twenty years, yet her body craved his desperately at the first touch. There was no way to reconcile that conflict. No way at all.

She drew herself up stiffly. "You shouldn't have come out here after me," she murmured. "You should have let me run."

He shook his head slowly. "You can't run from this."

"I have to."

"Michele—"

"I have to. I won't destroy my family, Ian. That price is too high; I can't pay it. There can't be anything between us. Not even peace."

"There *is* something between us. It isn't hate, and God knows it isn't peace, but it's real, Michele. You can't ignore it. And you can't run away from it."

"Watch me."

He swore under his breath, then said roughly, "And if I pulled you down in the sand right now? If I kissed you and touched you until you were holding on to me just the way you were a few minutes ago? Could you run then?"

With naked, simple honesty, she answered, "No."

He took half a step toward her, almost as if her admission had yanked at him, then stopped and held himself as stiffly as she. "But you'd hate me, wouldn't you?"

"I think I would." She felt tears sting her eyes and blinked them back. Her hands spread unconsciously in a gesture of helplessness, then fell. "Stay away from me, Ian. For both our sakes. For the sake of that torch we might be able to carry better than our fathers have."

"And that's it?"

Michele felt impossibly tired; her entire body ached dully with the throbbing echoes of what he had awakened in her. She nodded and turned away from him.

"Wait." He hesitated, then muttered an oath and shook his head as if he were at a loss. He reached into the pocket of his jacket and withdrew her small clutch bag. Holding it out to her, he said, "You left this at the table."

She accepted the purse automatically, and then kept walking back up the beach toward the hotel.

He didn't follow her.

She found her shoes near the door she'd run out earlier and picked them up without bothering to put them on. Her hose was ruined, she knew, and both sand and the residue of salt water clung to her feet and ankles. She didn't care. Ignoring the few curious stares she garnered in the lobby, she crossed to the elevators and rode up to her floor.

She felt immeasurably changed and numbly bewildered by the suddenness of it. Yesterday she had been confident and secure, her emotions on an even keel, virtually detached from the feud that had altered and ruined so many lives. But in only a few short hours, her detachment had been stripped away from her.

Her father had often been annoyed by her disinclination to join him in cursing the Stuarts, but he had shrugged away her lack of venom because he loved his daughter. Perhaps he even knew on some level that hate was a particularly ugly thing on the face of a woman. Still, it had never occurred to him that at the core of herself she didn't hate as strongly as he did. He simply expected it of her.

And she knew without a shadow of a doubt that if he discovered how close she had come to lying in the arms of his enemy, it would devastate him.

Michele had once thought the feud rather melodramatic, but her wry amusement had died on the day she'd first seen—really seen and understood—the depth of her father's hatred. She'd been no more than thirteen, becoming a woman with all the reluctance of a tomboy, and she'd fought her father fiercely when he had decided it was time for her to wear a dress and play hostess for some of his business dinners. Since her mother had died years before, he had been without a hostess, and Michele unwillingly had accepted that role.

Michele leaned against her door for a moment, then fumbled in her purse for the key and let herself into the room. She closed and locked the door and tossed her purse onto the bed, dropping her shoes on the floor.

It was during that first business dinner that a chance remark by one of the guests showed her the feud in a new and far more serious light. She had left the room for some reason, returning moments later and reaching the doorway just in time to hear the remark. She couldn't remember, now, the exact words, but one of the men had said something about how beautiful Charles Logan's daughter was going to be one day. She had paused, unexpectedly pleased. But then another man laughed and said something that had driven the pleasure away.

*"Stuart has a son just about the right age. That young man has a roving eye; take care it doesn't light on Michele. What perfect revenge that would be!"*

She had felt shock, and then she had seen her father's face and had understood what hate really was. His stony expression and the cold glitter in his eyes had been so dreadful that she had felt sickened by it. And even though his response had been uttered lightly, she had heard the implacable truth in it.

*"The day a Stuart lays a hand on my little girl is the last day he'll ever see. They won't even have to waste money burying him because I'll blow the bastard into a million pieces."*

She wasn't a little girl now, but she was still her father's daughter, and though the appalling truth that she had virtually invited seduction might possibly stop her father from getting his gun and going after Ian, nothing would prevent him from disowning her.

Ian was far less concerned by what a relationship between them would do to his father, she knew. Perhaps his father *was* less bitter. Or perhaps it was just that Ian knew what was, to Michele, a painful truth; a man could sleep with the daughter of an enemy and call it revenge. Or he could simply confess to a sexual attraction and shrug off who she was.

But a woman . . . no, it was different for a woman. To sleep with the son of her father's enemy would be the worst possible blow she could deal her father, and one from which he would never recover.

She was on the point of collapsing onto the bed when there was a sudden hammering on the connecting door to the next room, and a lively voice called out.

"Michele! Hey, open up—I made it!"

Jackie. Her best friend since childhood, and the one outsider who understood all too well the hatred between the Logans and the Stuarts. Orphaned and living with an aunt and uncle, Jackie had spent more time in Michele's home than in her own while they were growing up, and as a result, she had heard the Stuarts cursed for most of her life.

Michele glanced down at herself and then stepped to the mirror over the dresser. The reflection she saw made her wince. Her hair was tumbled wildly around a pale face, her lips swollen and reddened, her eyes holding a strained, darkened expression. But there was little she could do about her appearance; another bang on the door indicated that Jackie was waiting impatiently.

Opening her side of the connecting door, Michele deliberately spoke first. "When did you get here? I've been walking out on the beach."

Jackie looked her up and down, and then laughed. "No kidding. You look like hell, friend."

"Thanks a lot." Michele kept her voice light.

"As a matter of fact, the desk clerk told me he thought you'd gone out. I just got here a few minutes ago. Keep me company while I unpack, will you?"

"Let me take a shower first. I've got sand practically up to my knees."

"Okay," Jackie said amiably, turning back toward the open suitcases on the bed. "I guess you've eaten?"

"Uh huh." Had she? She couldn't remember. But she wasn't hungry.

"Well, I'm going to call down for something. The airplane food was the usual cooked cardboard. Want anything?"

"Not to eat. Some iced tea."

"I'll order it."

Michele retreated from the doorway. She got a sleep shirt from one of the dresser drawers and went into the bathroom. The bright light in that tiny room, unlike the shaded lamps of the bedroom, showed her even more clearly how she looked. Jackie had noticed nothing unusual, but Michele knew her friend too well to expect her to go on missing the obvious.

She stripped out of her clothing and took a long shower. When she got out, she dried off and wrapped her thick hair in a towel, then pulled the sleep shirt over her head. She was trying not to think, to keep her mind blank, but another glance in the mirror brought back vivid memories of Ian's kisses.

She *looked* kissed, thoroughly kissed, her lips faintly swollen and their color deeper than usual. She held a washcloth under cold water and then pressed the cloth to her mouth in an effort to erase the signs.

What she was doing sent a pang of bitterness through her. How dreadful to feel the need to wipe all evidence of a man's kisses from her face! Especially when she had invited those kisses and had responded wildly to them. Michele fiercely pushed the thoughts away.

Room service had come and gone, leaving a tray on the small table by Jackie's balcony doors. Michele took one of the chairs—the one out of direct light of the lamps—and poured herself a glass of tea, while Jackie took the other and began eating the club sandwich she'd ordered.

"So how's Martinique?" she asked cheerfully. "I

know you've already explored since you got here yesterday."

"It's just what the travel brochures promised. The scenery is gorgeous; wait until you see Mont Pelee. Fort-de-France has colorful houses and palms lining the streets. It's really beautiful."

"Well, since you were walking on the beach tonight, I gather the hotel has a respectable one?"

"So-so. It's only about half a mile long, and we're so close to the harbor that there's a lot of water traffic. But the hotel grounds have a lovely garden, and there's a big pool." She conjured a smile. "The service is good, the food's fine, the bed's comfortable, and rum is cheap."

Jackie giggled. "Neither of us likes rum."

"Well, it's cheap if we want any. In the meantime, we can lie on the beach or by the pool, and when we get tired of being lazy we can explore the island. I only got a quick look at it today, so there's plenty left to see."

"It sounds wonderful," Jackie said with a luxurious sigh. She was a redhead with bright green eyes and a vivid face. Full of life she seemed like a sister to Michele, who had loved her since they were children.

"A nice vacation. Speaking of which, I thought you were going to be held up a few days?"

"The crisis was resolved sooner than expected." Jackie grimaced. She was employed by one of the television stations in Atlanta, where crises occurred on a regular basis, especially in the news division where she worked as an assistant to a producer. "As soon as the dust settled, I told Doug I was gone and vanished before anything else could happen."

"He didn't waylay you at the airport?"

She grinned. "Obviously not. I'm here. I could have sworn I heard somebody calling my name in a pitiful voice as I escaped into the wild blue yonder."

"Leaving a note for Cole?"

Jackie's piquant face softened instantly at the name of the man in her life, but then her mouth twisted. "A message on his answering machine, dammit. He was out of town."

Michele hadn't yet met the paragon who had stolen her friend's heart, but she'd heard his name often enough during the past weeks.

"Where is he this time?"

"Lord knows. You'd think even a sales representative would know where he was going, but Cole never seems to. He barely had time to send me a dozen roses with a note. He said this trip would last only a couple of days, so I'll try calling him tomorrow. I wish he had been able to get time off. It would have been great."

"Thanks," Michele murmured.

Jackie cocked an eyebrow at her. "Not that you aren't loads of fun, but boasting a gorgeous man on my arm is definitely preferable to my childhood friend and roommate from college. Besides, I want to find out if he snores."

"You haven't yet?"

"Who's had time to sleep?" Jackie managed to look both deliriously happy and slightly self-conscious.

Michele felt a pang of envy, and instantly smothered it. Smiling, she said, "Then why on earth are you taking your vacation with your old college roommate? I know we planned this trip ages before you met Cole, but I would have understood—"

"I know, but he said he was going to be working long hours for a while, and I needed a break. Besides, Cole and I are too new to be making demands on each other. I don't want him to get the idea that I can't move a step without him."

"Just don't feel obligated to stay here with me."

"I won't." Jackie finished her sandwich and rose to resume her unpacking, adding in a calm tone, "By the way, what's happened to you?"

Michele sipped her tea to give herself a moment. "What do you mean?"

"Look in a mirror. I'd guess you've had some kind of shock. Obviously you're not going to volunteer any information, so I suppose I'm going to have to pull it out of you."

Michele had always confided in her friend. But this was something she couldn't confide to Jackie, who would never understand; she might not have Logan blood, but she had adopted the family and seemed to be convinced that a Stuart was the lowest animal on earth.

Michele felt very alone, trying to think of something that wouldn't be a lie—and wouldn't be the truth.

Jackie continued to unpack, but darted inquisitive glances at her oldest and closest friend. At last she said softly, "It must have been pretty bad."

Drawing a deep breath, Michele said, "I need to wrestle with it by myself for a while. Do you mind?"

"Your father and Jon are all right?"

"They're fine."

Jackie nodded. "Okay. Just don't forget I'm here when you're ready to talk about it."

"I won't."

After a long, thoughtful look at her friend, Jackie announced she was going to take a shower, and

Michele returned to her own room and moved around restlessly.

The ringing of the phone startled her. She frowned as she went to the bed and sat down, glancing at the clock on the nightstand before answering. Jon wouldn't call twice in one day unless . . .

"Hello?"

"Michele, don't hang up."

She felt her heart begin to pound, and swallowed hard. It was the first time she'd heard his voice over the phone, but she had no trouble recognizing it. "I wasn't going to," she said steadily. "I wanted to tell you something. Jackie got here a little while ago, so I'm not alone now."

"And you want me to stay away," Ian said flatly.

"I told you that on the beach."

He was silent for a moment, then sighed. "That isn't going to be easy, Michele. I meant what I said out there. I want you." His voice was low, and the last three words were a husky demand rather than a mere statement.

Michele leaned her head back against the headboard of the bed and closed her eyes. Why didn't she just hang up? She *should* hang up. Her pulse was racing and she felt hot. "Even if I knew I could trust you, it wouldn't be possible. Don't you understand?" Her breath caught as the haunting suspicions flooded up from the depths of her mind. "Or maybe you understand all too well."

"What's that supposed to mean?"

"Do you want to destroy my family, Ian, is that it? Is that what you're trying to do?"

"This isn't about our families, dammit, it's about us." His voice had sharpened and gone hard. "You and me, and what's between us  It doesn't have a thing to do with anyone else."

"You're wrong."

"No, I'm not. Twenty generations, Michele. Twenty generations of people living with hate and suspicion. Maybe you want to be part of that, but I don't. Your brother can hate me to hell and back, and I won't fight him. Do you understand that? I won't fight him. If I have to, I'll leave Atlanta, but the feud stops with me."

"Why?" She cleared her throat and steadied her voice. "Why are you so determined?"

His voice went low and rough again. "I held a Logan in my arms tonight. Maybe it never would have happened if we hadn't met in paradise, but it did happen. I can't be certain about much, Michele, but I know I could never hate you. So how could I hate your brother?"

Tears stung her eyes, but still she was remembering Jon's evasiveness earlier. What if something was happening, or about to happen, in Atlanta that would force Ian to hate? What if her father and Jon gave him no choice?

"Michele, please trust me. I won't do anything to hurt you, but I can't stay away."

She drew a shaky breath, fighting an intense longing. But clashing with that were suspicions and fears and the overwhelming knowledge that it just wasn't *possible*. "If you don't want to hurt me, you have to stay away. Good-bye, Ian." She cradled the receiver gently.


For three days, Ian stayed away. He made certain Jackie never caught a glimpse of him. He recognized the redhead as the one who, on the rare occasions he had been anywhere near her, had looked at him as if he were a leper. He had always felt more hostility coming from her than from Michele.

Still, he managed to watch Michele from time to time as she and her friend came and went. She was clearly bent on spending as little time at the hotel as possible, probably to keep away from him. But on the third day Jackie dragged her out to the pool, and Ian overheard the redhead laughingly say that she'd had enough sightseeing for a while and wanted to be lazy.

A slow anger built inside Ian when he saw Michele glance uneasily around. The hellish feud between their families had done this to her—and to him. A grown man and woman, attracted to each other yet fighting to ignore their feelings because they were supposed to be enemies.

Attracted? Lord, the word was useless to describe what he felt when he looked at her.

It had hit him only the night she'd hung up the telephone on him that he had wanted Michele Logan for a very long time. He had vivid memories of her at varying ages . . . and of his admiration for her talents and determination, as well as her beauty. He had known it somewhere deep inside him for years, but it wasn't something he had allowed himself to dwell on because the very idea had been unthinkable.

Until now. They were thousands of miles from home and the battleground both recognized; perhaps that had made it easier to consider the unthinkable. And after he'd held her in his arms, had been burned by the fire between them, the unthinkable had become the necessary.

Watching her during those three days, Ian went over and over it in his mind. He listed all the arguments against them, tried to see and understand that her risks would be greater than his, asked himself why he couldn't just forget this insanity.

But when he saw her just after dawn on the fourth day, he knew that he couldn't forget her, he couldn't let her run away, and he couldn't stay away.

The sun was barely up, hanging low and brilliantly orange over the island when he came out of the garden and caught sight of her on the strip of sand. The beach was deserted except for them. She was walking slowly along the waterline toward the place they'd stood when they'd kissed. And just as it had been before, he followed her without thought.

She reached the low ridge of volcanic rock, and this time climbed up a couple of feet and sat staring out at the sea. Her shining raven hair was hanging down her back in a simple braid, the end tied with a bit of lace. She was barefoot and wearing a white dress that made her look even more delicate and feminine than usual. The dress had a full skirt and thin straps tied on each of her shoulders.

She was unaware of his approach, and Ian reached her before she saw him. He felt his stomach tighten as he stepped up to her. He was standing literally between her legs; she had her feet braced apart on the rock, her skirt bunched up carelessly and draped between her thighs. They were nearly at eye level since he was still on the sand.

Michele's eyes widened, but she didn't say a word.

He didn't dare move closer; even without touching, their proximity and provocative positions charged the air between them. But he couldn't help lifting his hands and resting them lightly on her thighs, just above the knees and below the bunched folds of her white skirt.

"Where's your friend?" he murmured.

"She's sleeping in. She isn't a morning person."

"Have you been out here every morning? If so, I wish I'd known."

Michele cleared her throat softly. "I usually run in the mornings. I didn't feel like it today." She was trying not to shiver in pleasure as his thumbs rhythmically brushed the sensitive flesh of her inner thighs.

"I tried to stay away," Ian said roughly. "But I can't, Michele."

She started to push his hands off her but somehow couldn't complete the motion; the moment she touched him, it was as if her own strength drained away. She was throbbing for his touch.

He wanted to move fully into the cradle of her legs, to kiss her moist lips, to feel her in his arms again. The driving urge to lose himself in her until there was nothing on earth but the two of them and the fiery heat of mating was so powerful it filled his mind and sent a shudder through his body.

Her eyes closed suddenly and her slim hands gripped his wrists almost frantically. "I don't even trust you," she said in a voice that was nearly a moan. "Don't do this to me!"

Ian drew a deep breath and grimly hung on to his control. How could they sort through the tangle of thoughts and emotions when their physical response to each other was this explosive? It was almost impossible to think at all. He'd never wanted a woman so badly in his life, and it was clear that her need was just as great.

"Look at me, Michele," he ordered tautly.

She caught her breath, her lids lifting slowly to reveal shadowed, haunted eyes the color of a mountain fog.

"Let me teach you to trust me. Give me a chance. Give us a chance."

"Even if—" She broke off as he shook his head briefly.

"One step at a time," he urged, his voice still rough and strained. "We have to be sure. If you can't trust me, we'll never know how it could be between us. It'll end right here." He wondered if he had a hope in hell of keeping that promise when he could barely hold his own desire in check. "Please, Michele," he added softly.

She felt something inside her give way, deeper than the first wall that had crumbled the other night. And quite suddenly her mind was clear and quiet, the pain of indecision gone. As if she'd been straining against some irresistible pull and had finally let go and accepted the inevitable.

She gazed into those striking pale blue eyes, and her hands slowly relaxed their grip on his wrists. "All right," she said unsteadily. "Now what?"

Ian turned his hands to catch hers and stepped back, gently drawing her down to stand with him on the sand. "Now we try to get to know each other," he said.

Michele looked up at him, her fingers unconsciously clasping his. "I'll have to tell Jackie."

"How will she react?"

"Not well. She practically grew up in my house, so she's heard the Stuart name cursed most of her life. I'm not even sure she'll keep the confidence."

"She could call your father or brother?"

Michele shrugged. "I'll try to talk her out of that. I don't want them to know, Ian. I don't want to hurt either one of them if—if it isn't necessary."

He nodded, accepting that. "Why don't you both have breakfast with me? On that little terrace by the garden."

Not sure Jackie would even consent to sit at the same table with a Stuart, Michele managed an uncertain smile. "I'll ask her."

Ian held her hand as they began walking back toward the hotel. Striving for lightness, he said, "Tell her she can be watchdog, and protect you from the dragon."

# Three

Jackie Flynn leaned over the balcony railing and breathed in the morning air happily. She wasn't, by nature, a morning person, but this island life agreed with her, and she was finding it no hardship to rise earlier than usual. She was beginning to understand why Michele loved mornings. She was already up and about, probably running on the beach since that was her habit. Even on vacation, Michele wasn't the type to laze away her days.

Jackie leaned farther outward, peering to the left to try and catch a glimpse of the garden path to the beach, which was obscured by a wing of the building. She spotted Michele.

With a man.

A big blond man, Jackie noted with interest, and he was holding Michele's hand in a way that was possessive rather than casual. She watched them emerge from the garden and walk past the pool,

every step bringing them closer. Her smile faded, a
niggling uneasiness growing inside her. From her
position she could see Michele's face well, but only
the man's profile as he talked earnestly with her.

There was something about him. . . .

The conversation several floors below was finally
finished, and the man half turned to watch Michele
walk on alone. Jackie could see his face now, all too
clearly. She jerked back away from the railing, feeling sick.

"Oh, my God," she muttered.


Jackie was standing in the doorway to her room.

She looked pale, Michele thought, and her eyes
held a queer, stunned expression. "Jackie? Are you
all right?"

"I saw you." Jackie swallowed hard. "I saw you
with him."

Michele slowly crossed the room to the table by
the balcony doors and sat down in one of the chairs.
Her friend's extreme reaction didn't surprise her,
but it saddened her and made her think bitter
thoughts. Twenty years of poison had made Jackie
hate someone she didn't even know, someone who
had never lifted a hand against her, and that was a
terrible testament to the power of brainwashing.

"Tell me I didn't see that," Jackie begged, coming into the room and sinking down on the corner
of Michele's bed. "Tell me it wasn't Ian Stuart."

"It was."

"Michele . . ."

"I had car trouble the day after I got here,"
Michele said steadily. "He stopped to help me." Then
a touch of painful mockery entered her voice. "The

sky didn't fall, Jackie. I wasn't hit by a bolt of lightning. He didn't turn into a Medusa or a gorgon or Jack the Ripper. He just offered me a ride back here, and that night we had dinner together."

Jackie's piquant face was marred by her anguished expression. "Michele, he's a *Stuart*! He and his father have done their best to ruin your family for years—"

"No. Not Ian."

"Oh, and I suppose he told you that?"

Had he? He'd said that he wouldn't fight her brother, Michele remembered. That the feud would stop with him. But he hadn't actually denied any involvement in the past. She felt pricking little doubts creeping nearer and fiercely pushed them away.

"Jackie, try to understand. I didn't go looking for this; I didn't know he'd be here on the island. And the last thing I want to do is hurt Dad and Jon."

"But?" Jackie demanded sharply.

"Something happened that first night—"

"Did he hurt you?"

Michele shook her head, sighing. "No, nothing like that. It happened inside *me*, not because of anything he did. For the first time in my life, I—I felt like a woman. Everything came crashing in on me, so many emotions and needs and fears. It scared the hell out of me; I ran like a thief."

Jackie was staring at her, frowning. "Actually ran? Where?"

"Out on the beach."

"He followed you."

"Yes. And he knew why I was running, what I was running from. When he kissed me—"

"I knew it!" Jackie exclaimed, her normally pleasant voice hard. "The bastard's trying to seduce you!"

Michele felt a flash of sheer rage. "Is he?" she snapped back. "Then he missed a great opportunity that night, because I couldn't say no. I asked him *not* to stop!"

Jackie drew back a little and they stared at each other, shock on one face and anger on the other. It wasn't the first time they'd quarreled, but it was by far the most serious disagreement they had ever had.

"He's up to something," Jackie finally said, her tone unsteady. "He wants to hurt you, Michele."

"Why are you so sure of that? Because he's a Stuart? Does his name make him incapable of anything but hurt when it comes to me? Can it possibly be that he's just a man who happens to find me attractive?"

"Is that how it is with you?" Jackie asked. "Do you find him—attractive—because he's just a man? Do you feel that way in spite of his name, Michele? Or because of it?"

"What do you mean?"

"Forbidden fruit. It's supposed to taste sweeter."

Michele felt a jolt, the ugly little doubts creeping nearer again. Then she shook her head and muttered, "Nothing's that simple."

"Isn't it? Ian Stuart is the last man in the *world* you should get involved with. Your father would disown you in every sense of the word. So would Jon."

"I know that."

Jackie looked shocked again, and uneasy, as if she'd expected the reminder to cure her friend instantly of this madness. She stared for a moment, then said in a thin voice, "It would be a feather in his cap, wouldn't it? He could destroy your family and enjoy himself doing it. Make you care about him until nothing else mattered, until you broke your father's heart and—"

"That's enough." Michele tried to stifle her anger as she got to her feet and squared her shoulders. "You're my closest friend, Jackie, and I know you want what's best for me. So let me find out for myself what that is. Maybe it won't be Ian, but I have to make up my own mind. I can't hate him just because I've been told I should."

Jackie was silent for a moment, then asked stiffly, "I guess you expect me to keep my mouth shut about this?"

"To Dad and Jon? I hope you will." Michele slipped her feet into sandals and made sure her room key was still in the pocket of her skirt. "Maybe there won't be anything to tell them, in the end. But if there is, it should come from me."

Staring at the floor, Jackie said, "All right. I'll keep quiet. Maybe you'll come to your senses before they're hurt by this."

Michele went toward the door, then stopped and looked at her friend. "Ian's invited us for breakfast. Do you want to come?"

"I'm not hungry."

Not that she'd expected any other response. "We'll be at a table on the terrace if you change your mind." She was almost at the door when Jackie's quiet voice stopped her.

"Michele?"

"Yes?"

"He can hurt you so badly. He can hurt you more than any other man ever could."

There was nothing Michele could say to that, because it was the truth. Silently, she left the room and went to join Ian for breakfast.

"She didn't take it well," Ian noted a few minutes later.

Settled in her chair across from him in the morning sunshine, Michele conjured a faint smile. "Afraid
not. I can't even blame her for it, really. She's a
wonderful person, but she isn't any more rational
about you Stuarts than anyone in my family is."

"I suppose she pointed out all the reasons you
shouldn't see me again?"

"Oh, yes." Michele sighed. "All the reasons I'd
thought about and a few I hadn't." Then she shook
her head. "No, that isn't true. Jackie didn't say
anything I hadn't already said to myself. It just
sounded . . . worse coming from her."

Ian's jaw tightened. "I can imagine."

Michele glanced past him, then stiffened a bit.
"You won't have to. I guess she changed her mind."
Ian rose as Jackie moved toward them, and Michele
added in a low voice, "I hope you have a thick skin."

He certainly needed one, Ian decided during the
next hour or so. Jackie didn't hide her hostility one
bit, and if she could get a barbed comment in, she
didn't hesitate. Ian didn't mind for himself; it would
take more than the venom of this antagonistic redhead to make him lose his own temper. But he
minded for Michele, because he knew it bothered
her. She didn't say very much, hardly touched her
breakfast, and more than once angry color rose in
her cheeks.

The last thing Ian wanted to do was come between Michele and her friend; the cost of this relationship would likely be high enough without that
loss. But he couldn't bear to sit by and allow this
hate-filled young woman to tear their relationship to
pieces before it had a chance.

He signed the check, rose, then gently pulled Michele to her feet. "If you'll excuse us?" he said pleasantly to Jackie.

She ignored him, looking at her friend instead. "Jon'll probably call, Michele. Want me to tell him you're slumming?"

Evenly, Michele replied, "I never knew you were cruel, Jackie. Until now. Tell him any damn thing you want to." She turned away abruptly.

Ian saw Jackie's face whiten, but whether with anger or shame he couldn't say. He caught up with Michele in a few steps, and took her arm, guiding her back through the lobby and toward the front doors.

"Well, that little experiment was a mistake," he said wryly. "She hates my guts. And it isn't even her fight."

"I'm sorry." Michele's voice was low, her head bent.

He didn't reply until they were in his car and heading away from the hotel. "You don't have any reason to be sorry. Jackie's as much a victim of five hundred years as we are."

Michele half turned on the seat to look at him. "But we aren't reacting the same way. Why not? What makes you and me different?"

"Something stronger than both of us. Something that might even be stronger than the feud. That's what we have to find out, Michele."

The barbs Jackie had planted stung Michele's flesh . . . and she wondered what influence they would ultimately have on her relationship with Ian. All through breakfast, she'd been conscious of the aches of longing inside her, and every jab from Jackie had only made her more aware of it.

Gazing steadily at Ian now, she felt the longing intensify, numbing her doubts and suspicions. She wanted his arms wrapped around her, his mouth on hers, his hard body pressed against her. She wanted to forget that they were anything but a man and woman. Her wishes were so simple, so clear, so untroubled by any doubt, fear, distrust.

"Where are we going?" she asked huskily.

Ian sent her a quick glance, and a muscle leaped in his jaw as his hands tightened on the wheel. "Dammit, don't look at me like that," he warned in a taut voice.

It should have embarrassed her that her feelings showed so plainly on her face, but somehow it didn't. She was aware only of a tingling satisfaction that his response was so instant. "I can't help it," she murmured.

He drew a short breath, and the telltale muscle in his jaw flexed again as he stared straight ahead. "You'd better try, because it makes me want to drag you into the backseat like some horny teenager."

Michele tried to look away from him, but she couldn't. His blunt statement sent a stab of excitement through her, and the recklessness of that feeling pushed everything else out of her mind. She had to press her lips tightly together to keep herself from saying there was nothing she'd like more than to take him up on that rough promise.

Ian glanced at her again and instantly forced his attention back on the road. His brief look was enough to jerk the threads of his control painfully tight. He was going to plow the car into one of the palms lining the street if he wasn't careful, or else just pull over in front of someone's house and make love to her no matter who happened to stroll by. She was sitting there beside him in her prim white dress—except that it wasn't prim at all. The bodice had some kind of fishnet panels down both her sides and another in front, between her breasts; golden flesh was clearly visible through the net all the way to her slender waist. She wasn't wearing a bra; all he had to untie were the flimsy straps at her shoulders and smooth the sheer linen away to feel her naked breasts in his hands. The way she was looking at him only made matters worse. Her haunting gray eyes were soft and unfocused with the desire of a woman.

Ian cleared his throat harshly and held on to control with an iron grip. "Michele, for both our sakes, we have to be careful. If we become lovers before you trust me. . . ."

*Lovers.* The word made a wave of heat wash over her. To be Ian's lover, to lie in his arms, to feel his weight on her, to know his possession. That was what this was all about, she knew, what both of them had hesitated to name aloud. It was the connection that drew them together even though they were supposed to be on different sides of a war. Not rational or even sane, the compelling attraction existed, and they had to decide how best to deal with it.

She turned her head away finally, staring through the windshield, trying to gather her scattered wits. "Where are we going?" she repeated in a steadier voice.

"The waterfront park," he answered, his voice still a little strained. "I thought we could walk for a while. Talk."

"With lots of people around," she murmured.

"Lord knows I'd rather be alone with you. But I think we should avoid that."

Michele didn't protest his decision, even though a part of her wanted to. Ian was right. It was too dangerous for them to be alone, too tempting. She remained silent until they were walking slowly along one of the paths of the waterfront park. The place was busy with tourists, mostly American, but nonetheless it was a quiet and peaceful place.

"You said I was too honest to have hidden motives," she said, glancing up at him. "How can you be so sure? I mean, you must have listened to as many attacks on Logans as I have on Stuarts over the years."

"Attacks on Logans, yes," he admitted. "But always against your father and Jon. I don't believe my father ever said a thing against you personally. The closest he ever came was when he raked me over the coals when you beat me in that Grand Prix event ten years ago. He said I ought to be ashamed of myself for letting a Logan brat on a green horse beat me."

Michele couldn't help but smile. "I was determined to win that day—but not because you were a Stuart."

Rather dryly, Ian said, "I know. You were mad as hell at being dumped at my feet."

Startled, she said, "Yes, but how did you know that?"

He walked a few more steps in silence, then drew her hand through the crook of his arm. "It was in your eyes. Not hate, but something fierce and obstinate. As I remember, you had a few nasty things to say about my ancestors when I offered you a hand up, but that seemed more or less automatic."

She looked at her hand resting easily on his arm, with his hand lightly covering it. The offering of help she had furiously scorned at sixteen she had accepted the other day. And she wondered suddenly if anything would have been different had she accepted the first time.

"What are you thinking?" he asked.

Michele sighed. "What else?"

"It's never far away, is it?"

"It's not something either of us can forget. Ian, you said you wouldn't fight Jon. But have you? In the past, I mean?"

In a deliberate tone, Ian said, "I've never done anything against your father, your brother, or their company, Michele. I've never used an unfair business tactic to gain an advantage over them. Never."

"I had to ask," she said quietly.

"I know." His hand tightened over hers. "Let's make a bargain. No more talk about the feud, or our families for a while. We're two people getting to know each other, and that's all that matters now."

"I'll try."

"Good enough," he murmured.


They spent the entire day exploring the island. With all the caution of people walking a tightrope, they steered a careful course between the attraction they felt and the conflict of who they were. In getting to know each other, they discovered a surprising amount of common ground as well as a peculiar bond of understanding.

The latter, Michele thought, was certainly due to who they were. It was ironic, but the very threat to their relationship was also what enabled them to so quickly gain a sense of each other. They shared a unique background, a history linking their families for five centuries, and no matter how negative that link was, it was a powerful bond.

Michele was thinking of that as she unlocked her door early that evening. She and Ian had eaten lunch and dinner away from the hotel, not returning until late, and she wondered what Jackie had made of their extended absence.

The worst, no doubt.

The connecting door was closed on Jackie's side. Michele sighed but made no attempt to open it. Given her friend's present state of mind, there was really very little for them to say to each other. She went to take a shower, emerging a few minutes later dressed for bed in a sleep shirt.

"Michele?" Jackie was standing in the doorway to her room, wearing short pajamas and looking as if she'd been crying. "Can—can we talk? I have some iced tea in here."

Silently, Michele followed her friend into the other room, sitting down by the balcony doors and accepting a cold glass. "Did Jon call?" she asked.

"No."

Conscious of a niggling worry, Michele frowned at her glass. It wasn't that Jon called every single day, it was just that during his last few calls he'd been unusually silent about what was going on with the company—and the feud. He knew his sister had never approved of the "eye-for-an-eye" concept, and though he was quick to report some foul deed of the Stuarts, he was generally silent about what he and their father did in retaliation.

That was what had Michele concerned. Though Ian had denied any involvement in the troubles between their families, he had said nothing about his father, and Jon had seemed certain that a Stuart had been behind the company's recent problems—though that was, of course, his inevitable reaction to difficulties with the business. She couldn't help but feel uneasy about what might be happening in Atlanta, especially since she and Ian were trying to build a bridge instead of a fence.

"I'm sorry," Jackie blurted as she sank down on the bed and drew her legs up. "Sorry for the things I said, the way I acted this morning."

Michele was more than a little surprised. "That's quite a change of heart," she noted slowly. "Quite a *sudden* change of heart."

Jackie looked miserable. "I've been thinking about it all day. I'm your friend, Michele. I should be on your side no matter what. Lord knows nobody else is going to be."

"How can you be on my side? You hate Ian."

"No matter how I feel about him, I know how hard this has to be on you. I could see it on your face the other night. And you were right, it's your decision. It has to be. You aren't a child or an idiot. If your feelings for Ian are strong enough to overcome the fact that he's a Stuart, then—well, who am I to tell you it's wrong?"

Michele nodded, still surprised. "I'm glad you've changed your mind."

With a rather uncertain smile, Jackie said, "Hey, I know how tough a relationship can be with the normal number of strikes against it. You don't need me pointing out the obvious."

Michele sipped her tea, then said quietly, "You aren't giving us a snowball's chance in hell, are you?"

As quietly, Jackie said, "I can't lie to you, friend. I can't see a happy ending for this. We're thousands of miles from home, and maybe you *can* see Ian differently here. But back in Atlanta, he's a Stuart and you're a Logan. In Atlanta you're on opposite sides of a war. And sooner or later, you have to go back to your real world."

"Maybe we can go back together."

Jackie stared for a long moment, then leaned back on the bed. Her lips twitched in a sudden, rueful smile. "Well, if that happens, I want to watch. It ought to have about the same affect as Sherman's march through Atlanta."

In spite of her change of heart, Jackie turned down Ian's occasional invitations during the next two days. She was civil enough when she found herself in his presence but took care to avoid him. Michele accepted Jackie's limited support, then firmly closed her mind to all the problems that lay ahead. She also accepted Ian's determination to avoid the temptations of being alone together, and though it cost her sleepless nights she was even grateful for his resolution.

They explored the island, swam in the hotel's pool and walked on the beach—always with other people around. They shared meals and thoughts and opinions. They became familiar with each other's expressions and moods. Their closeness grew, and with it an ever-heightening sense of where their relationship was leading.

She had realized only in her early twenties that she had been ridiculously overprotected when it came to men. Since she'd been something of a tomboy, it hadn't disturbed her that her father had refused to allow her to date until her eighteenth birthday, or that her brother had found fault with every boy who'd expressed an interest in her. And she hadn't protested the situation simply because she hadn't been much interested in the dating scene.

It was only when she finished college and found a job that the reins had begun to feel uncomfortably tight. She continued to live at home because it *was* home, but also to avoid a fight with both her father and brother, and there definitely would have been a fight. Living under her father's roof, Michele felt she owed him the respect of conducting herself according to his rules. Perhaps because he felt the lack of a strong feminine influence in his daughter's life, Charles Logan had always been fierce about conventions—and his were decidedly old-fashioned.

The Logans were a family shaped by a Southern heritage, and Charles wasn't the only father of such a family who still harbored visions of Southern belles and gentility despite the realities of life in the final quarter of the twentieth century. He would have been shocked and deeply mortified if Michele had chosen to live openly with a man outside marriage. Though his remarks on the subject had been clumsily delivered during her early adolescence, his meaning had been clear; nice girls were virgins on their wedding nights.

And Michele Logan was a nice girl.


"You're very quiet."

They had spread beach towels on the sand just outside the garden and in the shade, away from the path of traffic to and from the beach. There were other hotel guests on the beach, but they were some distance away—visible, but not intrusive.

Michele set her book aside and rolled over on her stomach. She gazed toward the ocean rather than at Ian, wishing she had the nerve to dive into his arms and abandon everything else. Her doubts were growing rather than disappearing. She felt a sense of desperation, a painful feeling that she was going to lose something infinitely precious if she didn't act—and act quickly.

"*Can* I trust you?" she asked abruptly.

"I hope so."

She sat up and looked at him. They were both wearing bathing suits; he also wore a light windbreaker, and she a sheer linen caftan over her two-piece suit.

"After these past few days . . . I just don't know." Michele shook her head. "Does trust come in a blinding flash? Am I supposed to wake up one morning and say, 'Yes, today I trust Ian'? Or look at you and somehow know?"

"Michele—"

She felt tense, quivering on the edge of a chasm. "It isn't going to happen, Ian. You can't overcome twenty years in a week. That's all we have left, a week. Not even that, because your client is due here day after tomorrow. And I go home in seven days."

"What are you saying?" His voice was rough.

Michele struggled to find the words. "What happens when I go home? I'm no more certain of anything than I was the first day. I don't know if I can trust you. I don't even know if I trust myself to—to understand what I'm feeling. All I do know is that what we don't find here, we won't find in Atlanta."

Ian took a deep breath, aware that they had reached some kind of turning point. Michele had weighed it all in her mind, he knew, had wrestled with it in silence even while she'd walked beside him and smiled up at him and talked of other things.

She had struggled against a lifetime of conditioning and had ended up, now, certain of nothing except her uncertainties.

And it was an impasse; Ian didn't know what he could do to win her trust. Frustration gnawed at him, because he wanted Michele to the point of madness and she was held tauntingly out of his reach by a feud neither of them wanted any part of. He had pushed himself to the screaming limits of restraint when he wanted nothing more than to lock both of them in his room and shut out the world, and the waiting had him tied in knots.

"Ian?" She was gazing at him and felt a flutter as if something caged deep inside her sought escape. She'd never seen him look like this, his lean, handsome face hardening, his eyes containing a glitter that was hot and bright with a promise she instinctively understood. For an instant she was conscious of panic, but then heat rushed in to overwhelm her doubts and fears.

He leaned toward her, and Michele found herself being eased back onto the blanket. She felt the hardness of his thigh against hers, the strength of his arm under her. His head lowered, his mouth brushing hers very lightly, and his breath was warm.

"Maybe we haven't been looking in the right place," he muttered huskily.

Michele gazed up into those vivid eyes, smothered by the pounding of her heart, his first touch sending a dam-burst of sensations flooding through her body. The strength of her own feelings made her hands shake as they lifted to touch his face. "Maybe we haven't," she agreed in a whisper.

Ian made a low, rough sound and buried his face between her breasts. She caught her breath raggedly, her fingers sliding into his thick hair as she felt his mouth moving on her. The sheer material of her caftan was a frail barrier, but even that was too much, and he impatiently sought the warm flesh beneath. The first three big buttons down the front of the garment yielded, and he nuzzled between the lapels to find the curves of her breasts.

Michele's skimpy bathing suit was the final barrier, but Ian didn't try to remove it. His mouth slid along the cup of her bra, his tongue darting out to taste her silky skin. He felt her shudder, felt her fingers tighten in his hair as a smothered moan escaped her, and that soft, uncontrolled sound sent a jolt of frantic need through him.

"Yes?" he demanded thickly against her.

She moaned again, and her voice was so low it was hardly more than a whisper. "Yes . . . yes."

Ian raised his head and then kissed her deeply, molding his mouth to hers hungrily. Her response was instant, heated, her body arching against him wildly. He forced himself to remember where they were, and it was like fighting his way through a red-hot haze of necessity. Muttering a curse, he caught her hands and got to his feet, pulling her up.

"Ian?" Her voice was unsteady, bewildered.

"We're going up to my room," he said roughly. "Now."

Michele didn't protest. She couldn't have. She held on to Ian's hand like a lifeline, and even if her father and brother had been standing in the lobby, she wouldn't have paused or even hesitated. The need inside her was so strong it was like something with a life of its own, filling her until it could hardly be contained, until the pressure of it was almost unbearable. Was unbearable.

She didn't care what this cost her, what she lost because of it. Whatever price was demanded of her, she'd pay it.

In the elevator alone, Ian pulled her into his arms. "I'm not going to give you a chance to change your mind," he murmured, staring down at her with blazing eyes.

The fierce jolt of pleasure when Michele was pressed against his hard body made her catch her breath and close her eyes. Her arms slid up around his neck, and she stood on tiptoe to fit herself more intimately against him. "I don't want to change my mind," she whispered, all her emotions and senses fixed on him and nothing else.

Ian made a rough sound and lifted her into his arms as the elevator doors opened. He carried her down the hallway to his room. The maid was just coming out, and he brushed past the startled woman with an impatient, "Excuse us," kicking the door shut behind them.

A nervous giggle died in Michele's throat when he slowly lowered her to her feet beside the bed that lay in a bright spill of sunlight streaming in the balcony door. Her arms lowered, her hands trailing down between the edges of his partially unzipped windbreaker. His chest was hard, covered with a mat of thick golden hair that felt wonderfully sensual against her palms. She curled her fingers to probe the solid muscles beneath springy hair, aching to touch him all over. In the back of her mind was the vague thought that she really should tell him she'd never been with a man before, but the confession couldn't escape the tightness of her throat. She wanted this, wanted him, and nothing else seemed to matter.

"Michele . . ." He surrounded her upturned face in his hands and kissed her, his mouth warm and hard. She shivered as she felt the gliding touch of his tongue teasing the sensitive inner flesh of her lips, and opened her mouth wider under his in a mute plea for a deeper caress. Instantly he responded, his mouth slanting across hers, his tongue stroking hungrily against hers.

Dizziness washed over Michele in a hot wave. Desperate to touch him, she pulled at the windbreaker, hardly feeling the steel teeth of the zipper bite into her hands as she jerked the edges apart. He shrugged out of the garment and tossed it aside, then got rid of her caftan by simply yanking it open and pushing it off her shoulders. Without even thinking about it, she stepped out of her sandals and the pool of material at her feet, kicking them aside.

Gasping as his lips left hers, Michele felt his hands on her, moving over her back, unfastening the flimsy string ties of her top. She bit back a moan as the scrap of material was pulled off her and her naked breasts rubbed against his chest as she pressed herself closer. The fire inside her was burning out of control, her need so urgent she had to clench her teeth to hold back the wild, primitive cries she could feel rising in her throat.

Ian held her hard against him, his mouth buried in the warm flesh of her throat. She was so alive in his arms, so utterly responsive that he had no more control than a teenager. He wanted her with a burning fever that was worse than hunger, worse than thirst. Groaning harshly, he slid one arm down until it clamped below the swell of her bottom, then lifted her against him so that his face was buried between her breasts.

He could feel her heart thudding wildly, feel the sting of her nails digging into his shoulders. He explored the valley between her breasts, then slid his mouth hotly over a swelling curve and captured a tight nipple. She jerked, a whimpering sound escaping her as he sucked strongly.

Michele couldn't believe what she was feeling. His mouth on her breast sent pleasure stabbing along her nerve endings, and deep in her belly an awful ache throbbed emptily. She clung to him, almost sobbing at the shocks battering her senses.

"Ian . . ." Her voice was thin, shaking, her eyes closed tightly. "Ian, please . . ."

He shifted his hold on her slightly and bent forward to lay her on the bed, then straightened briefly to get rid of his shoes and trunks. Before Michele was fully aware of his absence, he was with her again. She felt his hands on her hips and lifted them instinctively as he stripped off what remained of her bathing suit and threw it aside.

Michele opened her eyes slowly, realizing that she was naked only when she saw him looking at her. A fleeting shyness vanished before it could take hold, because he was looking at her with such hunger it almost stopped her heart. She wouldn't have believed she could lie naked on a bed in a pool of bright sunlight while a man looked at her and feel only sharp excitement, but that was what she was feeling.

"Michele," he said tautly, kissing her deeply again and again before trailing his lips over her warm throat. His hand stroked her breasts, her quivering belly, then slid lower to gently probe the dark curls between her tense thighs.

She felt him touch her, and an explosion of

pleasure forced a gasp from her throat. Tension wound inside her with an almost brutal intensity, her control over her own body totally gone as it responded blindly, instinctively to the ancient mating drives. Her legs opened for him and she clutched at his shoulders desperately as his caress sent shockwaves of heat through her.

"Make it stop," she whispered raggedly, almost afraid of these wild feelings. "Ian, please . . ."

He drew a shuddering breath, fighting for a last remnant of control as he spread her legs wider and slipped between them. She was ready for him, her body warm and moist, her smoky eyes darkened and sleepy with desire. His own need was so wildly urgent he thought he'd explode, but he held himself back fiercely for the searing pleasure of entering her slowly.

It had never occurred to him that she might be a virgin; he'd seen men looking at her since she was sixteen, and given her sensual response to him, it seemed obvious that desire was something she had felt before. Even when her body resisted his slow entrance, the truth didn't hit him at once.

"Easy," he murmured, feeling a new tension tremble in her and seeing her eyes widen. He kissed her, holding her mouth with his hungrily as he bore down. He felt as well as heard the soft sound she made, and that was when he understood.

# Four

"Michele? Baby?" Ian felt as if he'd been kicked in the stomach, shock and something else jolting through him. And with that came a rush of hunger so intense he groaned aloud with it, shuddering as he fought to leash the wild urges of his body. He knew he'd never forgive himself if he hurt or frightened her, and it was only that knowledge that enabled him to find a measure of control.

She was looking up at him, her haunting eyes glimmering with wetness, her lips trembling. Slowly, the hands clutching his shoulders slid up around his neck, and her body moved tentatively beneath him. Her breath caught. "Ian?" she whispered.

He lowered his head and kissed her deeply, again and again until a kittenlike sound escaped her and she moved restlessly under him. Slowly, with exquisite care, he pressed deeper into her trembling body.

Michele was astonished at the sensations, dimly

shocked at the stark intimacy. She could feel her
flesh stretching to admit him, and then an increasing pressure that brought a flash of pain. Even with
that, she didn't want him to stop, because deeper
than the pain was an intolerable burning that cried
out for his complete possession. She hadn't realized
a man could be so strong, the male force of him
compelling her to accept whatever was necessary
because satisfying the need he had aroused in her
was all that mattered.

He was murmuring to her huskily, tender words
of comfort, kissing away the tears that trickled down
over her temples. Then she felt a sharper pain as
something gave way inside her, and even as she
cried out, she was conscious of nothing but a fierce
satisfaction. His heavy weight settled slowly, fully on
her, and the last whisper of pain ebbed as she felt
him throbbing inside her. It was an utterly alien
sensation, and yet she had never felt anything more
right.

"Michele?" He was braced on his forearms, his
eyes darkened to sapphire as they searched her face,
and his breathing was harsh and strained.

The hovering tension began spreading through
her again, and her arms tightened around his neck.
All the unfamiliar feelings tugged at her senses, and
she made an unconscious sound of pleasure. "Don't
stop," she whispered.

A hoarse groan rattled in Ian's chest as he briefly
considered the sheer impossibility of that. It would
kill him to stop now, to withdraw from the hot
velvety clasp of her body. Electric tremors shook his
muscles, and the ache in his loins was a pounding
torment. The strain of holding himself rigidly back
for so long was like floodwaters battering a dam,

and he knew he was a whisper away from going absolutely berserk.

He clamped his teeth together and began moving slowly inside her, aware on some dim level of his mind that he had never felt anything like this. The pleasure was unbelievable; his desire had reached a peak of sweet torment. His need for the woman whose slender body cradled his had gone beyond the point of madness; he felt consumed by it—and by her.

The soft sounds she made roused an almost primitive savagery in him, a fierce possessiveness as unfamiliar as it was powerful. She was *his*, he felt it with every fiber of his being. He wanted to bury himself in her, to fuse their bodies until nothing this side of death could ever separate them.

Michele felt that wild need take hold of her again, gripping her mind and senses so tightly that she could only give in to instinct. Her body knew how to match his rhythm, how to give itself totally to him and the fiery desire between them. The feelings rose in her like a tide, a force of nature she had no hope of fighting or controlling. She said his name over and over, barely aware that she was crying again, that she was straining to reach some unimaginable place. And then she was there with a suddenness that stole what was left of her breath, violent waves of shattering pleasure thundering over her as a soundless wail tore free inside her.

Ian held her strongly as she writhed under him, the internal shudders of her ecstasy caressing him with a stark pleasure that was agony. The final fragile thread of his control snapped, and he drove into her wildly, blind and deaf to everything except the woman in his arms and the exploding force of his release.

Michele felt herself floating for what seemed like a long time, her body limp and sated. She was gradually aware of her surroundings, of his heavy weight, of dim aftershocks somewhere deep inside her. He was still with her, and she loved the stark intimacy of that sensation. She loved the feeling of his hard body covering hers, the smooth strength of his hips against the insides of her thighs, the mat of hair on his chest sensual against her breasts. She loved the way the muscles of his back and shoulders felt under her probing touch.

She loved him.

It should have come as a shock, that realization, but instead it crept gently into her mind and settled there as if a place had been made for it long ago. She understood, now, why her need for him had been so great, why she had taken fire at his simplest touch and offered herself to him without hesitation. She loved him. He was the last man in the world she should have loved, and the odds against them were so great it was terrifying, but none of that mattered right now.

She loved him. And she let herself luxuriate in that strange and wonderful new feeling without counting the cost of it.

Ian pushed himself up on his elbows, his eyes still darkened as they gazed down at her. "I'm sorry I hurt you, baby," he murmured huskily.

Michele had a vague memory of pain, but it didn't seem important; like all pain, once gone it became only a word. She lifted her head to kiss him, then smiled.

He felt his heart lurch, the curve of her lips and

the misty depths of her eyes getting to him in some mysterious way he couldn't even name. "You should have told me," he said, hearing the rasp of his voice.

"Why?" she asked softly. "Would you have stopped?"

He half closed his eyes. "I couldn't have stopped if the roof had caved in on us," he told her. "Lord, Michele, you had me so crazy I hardly knew what I was doing."

"You did just fine," she assured him solemnly.

He couldn't help but smile, his worry about having hurt her fading in the knowledge of her obvious pleasure and contentment. He kissed her gently, then began to ease away.

Her legs tightened. "Don't go. I like you there."

"I like me here too. But I'm too heavy for you."

She shook her head slightly, her arms remaining securely around his neck. "No, you aren't." Her eyes were closing, and her voice was fading a bit. "Stay with me."

Ian knew she was drifting off to sleep, the culmination of days of tension and their fierce lovemaking having the inevitable effect on her. He was exhausted himself, but had no intention of giving way to sleep while she bore his weight. Despite her assurances, he knew he was too heavy to lie for long on her petite body.

So he kept his upper body braced on his arms and waited for sleep to envelop her completely. During those moments, he gazed down at her, very conscious of the fact that his desire had been merely blunted. Even now, as physically weary as he was, he could feel faint stirrings, tremors in his flesh, that told him another wave of need was not far off.

She seemed almost fragile as she cradled him in sleep, her slender, small-boned frame an exquisite

but delicate vessel for the fiery passions that had
blazed inside her with such unexpected and mes-
merizing force. In her innocence, she'd been obviously surprised at the sensations of joining, yet totally
involved in what was happening between them. Her
capacity to give and receive pleasure was heart-
stopping in its uninhibited simplicity.

Ian brushed a strand of silky black hair away
from her temple, feeling his pulse quicken and the
stirrings in his loins intensify. She was so beautiful,
so wildly exciting.

The enormity of what they'd done swept over
him, even though he tried to push the realization
out of his mind. Carefully, he eased away from her,
and when she murmured in sleepy protest gathered
her into his arms. She immediately cuddled closer
to his side, her peaceful sigh warm against his skin.

His own longing for sleep had vanished, chased
away by the renewal of desire or by his disquieting
thoughts. From the beginning, he had refused to
look further than the present, intent on exploring
what lay between them, defining it, forcing her to
accept the reality of it. He had called it passion, but
he knew it was more.

He also knew, only too well, that what could
flourish in paradise would be brutally attacked in
the real world. And the men who would attack it, his
father and Michele's especially, were experts in the
destructive art of warfare. They'd give no quarter,
either of them, no mercy even to their children.

Ian's arms tightened around Michele as, finally
and completely, he faced the truth of what they were
up against. It wasn't words now; it wasn't some far
off "what if," an abstract battle that would be fought
only if their rational minds weighed the risks and

counted the struggle worthwhile. The time for deciding had long passed—if it had existed at all.

Maybe they'd never had a choice.

Michele was only vaguely aware of discomfort at first. She felt hot and sticky, and the brightness seeping behind her closed eyelids was annoying. Her internal clock told her it was the middle of the afternoon, and she wondered dimly why she was trying to sleep at such a ridiculous time of day. She shifted restlessly and abruptly felt trapped by something hard.

Her first impulse was to escape, but even as she lifted her head, she remembered where she was. And whom she was with. She opened her eyes, blinking at the brightness; the sunlight was really pouring in now, and no breeze found its way through the open balcony door to disturb the hot stillness.

Ian was looking at her gravely, both his arms holding her securely. "Hi."

*I am lying naked*, she thought, wondering if she was supposed to feel shocked by that. *I am lying naked on a fully made bed in the sunlight with a naked man.*

She felt her lips twitch and smothered an absurd impulse to giggle. "Hi. Is it my imagination, or is it awfully hot in here?"

"It's awfully hot. The air conditioner isn't on." His arms tightened briefly around her, and then he slid from the bed, totally unconcerned by his nudity, and picked her up.

"I can walk," she noted idly, wondering if she could.

He kissed her, then turned toward the bathroom, ignoring her mild objection. He carried her into the small room, opened the shower stall and set her on her feet inside, then joined her and closed the door behind them.

Michele was feeling a bit unnerved by the sheer size of him in the small cubicle, and she was completely unprepared for the sudden blast of cool water over her heated skin. "Damn!" she gasped, pushing soaked hair out of her face and wondering when her braid had come undone.

Ian chuckled and kissed her briefly. "We need to cool off," he said blandly.

"You could have warned me before you turned on the water," she said, but it was only a murmur. Too overwhelmed by desire before, she hadn't really looked at his body; she couldn't help but look now, and what she saw fascinated her. She'd known he was big, but naked and enclosed with her in the shower stall his size and raw strength were compelling. He had the hard muscles of a construction worker rather than an architect, rippling under taut bronze skin. The thick mat of blond hair on his broad chest arrowed downward over his flat stomach, and as her gaze followed that path her mouth went dry.

"I think you had your eyes closed before," he said, the words light, his voice deep.

She felt heat from a new source rise in her cheeks, but there was also a sharp stab of excitement at the knowledge that he was becoming aroused by her scrutiny. "I must have," she admitted, meeting his darkened eyes a little shyly.

He smiled, then pulled her toward him a step, gently turned her so that her back was to him, and reached for a small bottle of shampoo to begin washing her hair.

Michele purred with pleasure. His long fingers felt wonderful moving over her scalp; at first the touch was soothing, but slowly tension spread through her. She could feel her heart thudding hard, her breathing grow shallow. Obeying his touch, she turned again as he rinsed the lather from her hair.

His face was still, eyes very intent on her. He reached up to angle the stream of water slightly away from them, then picked up a bar of soap from the corner ledge of the stall and very slowly began washing her body.

Michele was still surprised that she felt no self-consciousness or embarrassment. It had to be due to Ian—the way he looked at her body, the way he touched her, made her feel beautiful and desired, made her feel proud that he found such pleasure in her. His hands stroked over her breasts gently, tracing their shape, brushing lightly over the tight nipples in a touch that brought fire to her sensitive skin. Then, with agonizing slowness, he slid a soapy hand down over her belly and between her thighs.

She gasped and reached for his shoulders to steady herself as her legs went weak and shaky, all her consciousness focused totally on what he was doing. The faint soreness she'd hardly been aware of became a different kind of ache, one she could barely endure. Hunger filled her; throbbing heat radiated outward from the core of her. His fingers probed gently, sending hot shivers of desire singing through her veins until she whimpered with the force of it.

Ian made a rough sound and then slowly withdrew his hand, sliding it over her hip and around to shape the curve of her buttock. "Easy," he muttered, his face taut, and seemed to be telling himself that as well as her.

"Why?"

His eyes flared at the urgent protest of her voice, and he swallowed hard. "I don't want to hurt you again. You'll be sore, baby, you need time."

The only pain Michele was aware of was the burning ache she knew he could satisfy. Consumed by the sudden need to touch him, she took the soap and began sliding it over his hairy chest until she worked up a lather, then dropped the bar back onto the ledge. She explored slowly, touching him the way she wanted to, delighting in the feel of him. Her fingers brushed the hard nubs of his nipples, and when he shuddered she felt her own excitement spiral wildly.

"Michele . . ."

The taut warning had no power to stop her, and even the unexpected sensuality of her own nature was little more than a dim and unimportant shock. His stomach was flat and hard, his hips smooth, his thighs powerful. She could see the effect her touch was having on him, and it was both reassuring and unbelievably thrilling to know that he could no more resist her than she could resist him.

With curiosity as well as need driving her, she felt compelled to learn every part of his body. She had taken him inside her, and yet she hadn't touched him, not like this, and the urge to go on touching him was overpowering. Barely aware of his harsh breathing, she moved her slippery hands back up his thighs and very gently closed her fingers around him. She felt him jerk slightly and heard the rough groan that rumbled in his chest, and his response only spurred her on. His flesh was hard in her hand, pulsing with living need, and everything inside her seemed to dissolve into a hot liquid pool of desire as she touched him.

"Lord," Ian muttered hoarsely, pulling her into his arms. The force of his sudden movement put them under the shower spray, and the water streamed over them as he covered her wet mouth hungrily with his. He wanted her so desperately that he didn't have the will to get them out of the stall; even the few steps necessary were totally beyond him. Touching her had strained his control to the limits; her delicate hands on him were more than he could stand.

Her arms went up around his neck and she pressed her wet body to him, whimpers of intolerable desire tangling in her throat. She was on the raw edge of tension, so ready for him that waiting even a moment was impossible. She felt the cool tile of the wall at her back, and her legs parted as his hands slid down to her bottom.

She felt herself being lifted, felt a blunt pressure against her aching flesh, and then the burning sweetness of his invasion. Her legs locked around him strongly as she drew him even deeper into her softness, and the tension inside her snapped with a violence that made her moan into his mouth. His deep thrusts held her at the searing peak of pleasure, her body shuddering under the assault on her senses.

Ian was hardly aware of the sounds escaping his tight throat or of anything except the shattering sensations. She was writhing against him, her silky flesh so tight and hot around him, the waves of her pleasure caressing him with a sweet agony that pushed him wildly over the brink into a heart-stopping release.

Michele felt so utterly drained that she could only bury her face against his throat as her legs finally slid down his. She could feel his heart thudding against her, and when their bodies slowly disengaged she sighed with a mixture of satisfaction and regret.

"Lord, Michele," Ian said huskily, tangling his fingers in her wet hair and pulling her head back gently so he could kiss her. His lips brushed hers warmly.

She smiled at him, then said idly, "We're in the shower."

"And we could have broken our necks."

"Maybe we'd better get out, then."

The reasonable comment struck him as amusing. After the acrobatics of moments ago, he doubted they were in danger by just standing in the stall. But he obediently turned off the water and opened the door.

A few moments later, wrapped in one towel and drying her hair with another, Michele sat on the edge of the bed and gazed down at their clothing scattered on the floor. "I don't have anything to wear," she said, "except for a bathing suit and a caftan without any buttons. Did you do that?"

"Don't you remember?" he asked, pulling on a pair of jeans.

"Well, no. Not that it matters. I can always hold the edges together."

Ian came to the bed and sat down beside her. "You don't need anything to wear. Stay with me."

She finger-combed her damp hair and looked at him uncertainly. "Tonight?"

"And tomorrow night. And as many nights as we can manage." He kept his voice light.

"All right," she said simply.

"We have to talk."

A shadow crossed her eyes. "I don't want to talk."

He eased her back onto the bed and kissed her gently. "Baby, we have to. You know we do."

The faintly swollen curve of her lips was unsteady for a moment, then firmed. In her eyes was anxiety and reluctance and regret. "Yes. I know."

"We'll work it out," he promised, pushing from his mind the certain knowledge that there was no painless solution. "Why don't you call room service and order some food. I'll be right back."

"Where are you going?"

His smile went a little crooked. "Unless you're on the pill, I'm going to that shop in the lobby."

Michele felt herself blushing, which was, she told herself, fiercely ridiculous. "Oh."

He kissed her again. "I've been so wild for you I didn't even think about protection. I'm sorry."

"I didn't think about it either," she reminded him.

His eyes burned down at her, and one hand rested possessively over her stomach. "We may be too late," he said gruffly.

The possibility of carrying his child sent a surge of warmth spreading through her. But she wasn't certain of his feelings even now; as wild as their desire for each other was, he'd said nothing about their future. And the odds were so strong against them. . . .

Conjuring a smile, she said ruefully, "Stuart seed taking root in a Logan? Our ancestors would be spinning in their graves."

"And our fathers foaming at the mouth," Ian added. "Still, unlikelier things have happened."

"I know."

He hesitated, then kissed her lightly. "Whatever happens, we'll face it together."

After he'd finished dressing and gone, Michele rose and found a shirt in his closet. She put it on and borrowed his comb to untangle her damp hair, then called room service and ordered food to be sent up. She picked their scattered clothing up off the floor. Then, after a slight hesitation, she called down to Jackie's room. Her friend answered on the first ring.

"Hi, it's me," Michele said.

"Hello, stranger," Jackie replied dryly.

"I just wanted you to know that I—I'm going to be with Ian for a while. Didn't want you to worry."

There was a long pause, and then Jackie said, "So. You're lovers." Her voice was flat.

"Does that surprise you?"

"No. No, it doesn't surprise me. Jon called a little while ago. I told him you were fine, and out on the beach. I don't like lying, Michele."

"You weren't lying. I am fine."

"If you say so." Jackie's voice was still flat and polite.

Michele sighed and gave up. "I'll talk to you later, all right?"

"Sure."

After hanging up the phone, Michele continued to sit on the bed, gazing at nothing. Jackie's reaction had been only a sample, a mild sample at that, of what awaited her in Atlanta. She hadn't wanted to think about that; in Ian's arms, she'd been able to forget.

But she couldn't forget for long. She loved Ian—

but did she trust him? Even now, even after all they'd shared, she didn't have that answer. Alone in his room without the sight and touch of him to send every rational thought spinning into oblivion, she felt wary, uncertain, painfully vulnerable. And in the back of her mind were dark stirrings she couldn't seem to banish. Jackie had been right; Ian could hurt her more dreadfully than any other man.

For herself, she had no choice but to accept that possibility. The greatest shock of her love for Ian wasn't that he was her family's enemy, or that she went wild in his arms with a passion she hadn't known herself capable of. The greatest shock was the complete disappearance of her pride. She'd been raised to be proud, that being the single surviving trait of a Southern heritage; raised by a man whose pride in his name and in his person was immense.

But her love for Ian put such arrogance in perspective. Because she loved, she was achingly vulnerable, and that lowering of all barriers left her with the knowledge that pride didn't matter. As long as he wanted her, she belonged to him. For the rest of her life, she belonged to him.

For herself, it didn't matter who he was. But her father and brother would never see it that way. And along with her own natural uncertainties and doubts at accepting a man as her lover, she had to cope with the terrible knowledge that her relationship with Ian could be the spark that would ignite violence between their families.

"Are you decent?"

Startled, she looked up and saw Ian peering at her around the partially opened door. She hadn't even heard his key in the lock. "Of course I'm de-

cent," she said, pushing her anxiety back into its
dark corner.

He looked at her thoughtfully, then said, "No,"
and disappeared. Moments later, he opened the door
all the way and pushed a room service cart in ahead
of him. "Decent enough for me," he said calmly,
"but not the waiter."

"I'm wearing clothes."

"You're wearing my shirt—and you look sexy as
hell in it. Have I told you you're beautiful?"

"Umm . . . I don't remember."

"I must have been saying it inside my head,
then. You are beautiful." Ian was concentrating on
shifting the food from the cart onto the table by his
balcony door. "I thought so when you were sixteen."

"What?" That really did surprise her.

He pushed the emptied cart back out into the
hall and then came back and shut the door. He
came to the bed and drew her to her feet, enfolding
her in his arms. "Now why does that surprise you so
much?"

Michele blinked up into his smiling face. "Well, I
was gawky. All bones."

"All lovely bones. And wild hair and haunting
eyes. You've been in my head ever since, like a song I
couldn't forget. I used to catch a glimpse of you
across some huge, crowded room, a theater lobby,
or restaurant, and I'd wonder what would happen if
I went up to you, considering the curses you'd spit
at me when you were sixteen—"

"I wouldn't have," she murmured, realizing that
it was true.

Ian kissed her, holding her hard for a moment.
Then he guided her to the table and put her in one
of the chairs while he took the other. "We better eat

to keep up our strength," he said in a slightly rough voice. He looked at her, his eyes burning.

Reading the heated expression correctly, Michele felt a jolt of desire. Lord, just a look from him and she went weak. She fixed her gaze on her plate, concentrating on eating even though she'd forgotten what she'd ordered.

Ian ate automatically, hardly able to keep his eyes off her. She looked so delicate enveloped in his shirt, the dark cloud of her hair making her appear almost sixteen again. He knew she was troubled, knew that during his absence she had begun to confront what lay ahead of them. And he also knew that if he took her in his arms, she'd forget the problems. For a while.

The desire between them pushed everything else away, leaving only them and what they felt. But with the sharp edge of that blunted, however momentarily, the world and the problems outside crept closer.

In a low voice, without looking up, she said, "Do you think we can stop the feud?"

"I don't know." He wished he had a better answer.

She looked up then, gray eyes clouded. "Between our fathers, it's always stopped short of violence. Have you realized that—our relationship could change that?"

"We won't let it happen, Michele."

"How will we stop it? By telling them it's just us, that they aren't involved? They won't see it that way. By telling them we didn't plan this? That won't matter. They won't understand, Ian. They'll never understand."

He was silent for a moment, then pushed his plate away and sat back. Reluctantly, he said, "It'll be worse on you, even assuming we can keep them from striking out at each other. No matter how furious my father is, he won't disown me. I'm his only son, the last of the line."

Michele shivered almost unconsciously. "Dad . . . won't be that rational. I'd be lucky if he gave me time to pack. Years ago, I heard him say what he'd do if a Stuart ever touched me. I saw the look in his eyes. I'm afraid of what he might do to you and your father."

"Michele . . ." He reached across the small table and covered one of her hands with his.

"I don't even know how to tell him. Or Jon." Her hand turned under his, holding on as if to a lifeline. "I think I'm more afraid of what Jon will do. He's always been very protective of me—and he hates you."

"But he loves you," Ian said quietly. "So does your father. I can't believe either of them would hurt you." Even though part of his mind was telling him she was right, that her family could very well react with a violence that would catch her in its storm, another part of him found it impossible that any man could look into her eyes and say or do anything to hurt her.

Michele pulled her hand away and met his gaze very steadily. "Can't you? Do you want me to tell you how they'll look at this, what they'll say? They'll say that you set out to make a fool of me, that you cold-bloodedly seduced me with the intention of tearing our family apart. They'll say you used me as a tool or a weapon to further delay the completion of Dad's building, that you wanted to—to disrupt our family any and every way you could, put us at each other's throats—"

"Michele—"

She rose jerkily and stepped away from the table, away from the sudden dark realization in his eyes. She leaned against the open balcony door and stared out on paradise. "That's what they'll say," she whispered.

"And that's what you think, isn't it?" Ian rose as well, going to her and turning her around roughly to face him. "My Lord, you still don't trust me."

She stared at the pulse beating in his neck, unable to meet his eyes. "I can't get it out of my head," she said unsteadily. "The words. All the awful things I've heard for twenty years. I try not to— but I keep hearing them. And I know what it'll do to Dad and Jon, I *know*. I'm the best weapon you could use to destroy them."

"Even now?" His voice was tight. "Even now, you think I'm using you?"

Feeling the hot sting of tears, she looked up finally into his hard face. "I don't want to. Don't you see, Ian? When you hold me, it doesn't matter because it's just us and I know I have to take the chance. I can't fight what you make me feel."

"But you can't trust me not to destroy your family."

She saw her hands go up, saw them touch his face in some aching effort to soften him. But the touch seemed to go unfelt, his expression remaining hard and his eyes flinty. Despair swept over her as she tried to make him see and understand the pain tearing at her.

"Please . . . You made me face this. You said we had to talk about it. I'm trying to tell you that no matter how strongly you make me feel, and even though I could never hate you, I still can't forget what I've been taught. And if *I* can't forget that, if I can't trust you with all that I feel, after everything that's happened between us, then how could my family ever survive this? Ian . . . what we *are* will destroy them."

He pulled her suddenly into his arms, holding her as if something had tried to snatch her away from him. He hadn't wanted to face the fact that it could never, ever, be just them, that what they felt for each other couldn't be held separate and apart from the feud between their families. But he had to accept it now. They were each bound by ties of blood and love to opposite sides of a battle that had raged for centuries, and no bond between them, by the simple fact of its existence, could end that war.

His father wouldn't disown him, but the bitterness and sense of betrayal would always be between them. And her father and brother would never be able to accept him in Michele's life. Not with the feud raging stronger than ever between the families.

"We'll find a way to stop it," he muttered into the dark silk of her hair. His arms tightened around her, and he lifted his head to stare down at her. "Somehow. We won't let it destroy them—or us."

Michele let herself be comforted by his certainty, because the alternative was simply too painful. In any case, there was no going back. She pushed all the horrible words back into their darkness, and with their banishment came the sharp awakening of everything else she felt for him. The desire rising in her with such abruptness held more than a little desperation and she knew it, but she didn't care. These feelings were honest and untainted by dark things; these feelings were all she could really be sure of between them.

"I want you," she whispered.

His breath caught as she pressed closer, and his eyes flared with instant heat as his head bent to hers. "Michele," he murmured against her lips. "Michele . . ."

Late the following morning, Ian swore creatively as he dressed, his feelings obvious. "It isn't enough that the client has to arrive a day early," he said irritably, "but then he has the nerve to ask me to meet him on the other end of the island and spend the day walking over the job site."

"It can't be helped," Michele said, lying on her side in bed as she watched him.

"Come with me."

"Do you really think that would be wise?" she murmured.

Ian looked at her, lying in his bed naked except for the sheet draped over her, and he knew exactly what she was thinking. They had decided to eat dinner downstairs in the restaurant the night before. They'd stopped by her room so that Michele could put on something besides a caftan with no buttons, and then had gone on to the restaurant.

They hadn't made it to dessert.

Smiling just a little with a smile that was pleased and secret and so intimate it nearly made his heart stop, she said, "Your client probably wouldn't be thrilled to watch us vanish into the bushes."

He leaned over the bed, placing a hand on either side of her. "Do you think that would happen?"

"You tell me."

Ian knew damned well it would; in the last twenty-four hours, touching her had become as necessary as breathing, and since her desire was as strong as his, those touches just couldn't be casual ones. "You make me feel eighteen and at the mercy of my hormones," he told her.

"Good." Smiling, she lifted her face for his kiss.

"Dammit. I hate to leave you," he murmured against her mouth, thinking that if he ever saw her smile like that at another man, he'd kill the bastard. The primitive impulses and urges he felt around her no longer surprised him, for he'd learned the simple truth about himself: He was a man deeply, possessively, and irrevocably in love.

She sighed regretfully as he straightened, then said, "Just for a few hours. I should spend some time with Jackie anyway. Call home. Things like that."

"I'll be back before six. No matter what the client says."

"All right. I'll be here or in my room."

After he'd gone, Michele stretched like a lazy cat and reluctantly got up. She wanted to hold on to the peaceful feeling of well-being as long as possible, and determinedly kept her mind sedate as she dressed in the clothing that had been very hastily abandoned the night before.

The memory brought a smile to her lips as she left his room and slipped downstairs to her own to shower and change, but the smile left her as Jackie's closed door reminded Michele of things she wanted to forget. After the brief but painful discussion between her and Ian yesterday, neither of them had wanted to return to the subject of their future, and so it had been left hanging.

Michele still didn't want to think about it. She knew the problems wouldn't vanish by being ignored, but the wonderful hours with Ian and the delight she had found in his arms was an interlude she wasn't yet ready to jeopardize in any way.

She was dressed and brushing her drying hair when Jackie suddenly appeared in the connecting doorway.

"Hi. Abandoned so soon?"

Looking at her friend, Michele wished she could say something to ease Jackie's worry; her studied unconcern and flippant tone didn't hide her anxiety. "Ian had to meet a client on the other side of the island."

Jackie came far enough into the room to lean a hip on the low dresser. "Oh. So you're at loose ends?"

"For a few hours anyway."

"Then let's go have our fortunes read."

Michele wasn't surprised by the suggestion. Jackie's interest in fortune telling was a long-standing one; since her early teens she'd been dragging various of her friends to palmists, tarot card readers, and psychics. She had collected her share of futures, most of them containing the invariable promise of a tall, dark, and handsome man—and the fact that the man she had recently become involved with could easily fit that description had only deepened her faith in destiny.

It wasn't a belief Michele ever shared. Humoring Jackie, she'd gone along and had her fortune read a number of times. She, too, had been promised a tall, dark stranger in her future. One enthusiastic palmist had even told her flatly that her first lover would be a dark man with burning eyes.

Well, Michele thought now with a flash of amusement, she'd gotten it half right.

Mildly, she said, "I'm game. Have you already found a fortune teller on the island?"

Jackie drew a card from the back pocket of her jeans and looked at it. "This was pushed under my door this morning. There's some kind of small carnival out by the harbor, just for the day. And a Mrs. Fortune offers tarot readings."

Wondering idly why there had been no card under her own door or Ian's, Michele came to the conclusion that Mrs. Fortune no doubt had a limited supply of cards; most of her breed made a marginal living at best. Luckily she had shoved one under the door of a true believer in fortune telling.

"Okay," she agreed. "Are you hoping you'll get a prediction of when Cole will propose?"

"This time," Jackie said lightly, "I'm not so much interested in my future. It's yours I'm wondering about."

# Five

The carnival was like most that Michele had seen in the States. There were a few rides for children, a number of exhibits and games, and the place was packed. The only obvious difference was that the carnies here called out to customers in three languages. Most of the patrons were tourists, a large majority American, all clearly willing to accept the games as honest, the exhibits as containing at least a reasonable facsimile of what was so luridly painted on the outside of the tents, and the rides as safe.

Mrs. Fortune's tent was surprisingly subdued, given its atmospheric background. It was a soft violet in color, and boasted only a sign in Old English script above the tent flap promising that tarot readings were conducted inside. Outside and to the right of the opening stood a man, and he made no effort to try and entice the milling tourists to enter the tent. He merely studied the crowd, occasionally smiling or nodding if someone looked his way.

Jackie, who had no interest in anything other than a possible glimpse into her friend's future, had Michele by the arm and was leading her inexorably to the tent.

Michele had accepted her fate, but as they drew near the man outside the tent, she found her whole attention focused on him. He was certainly a fascinating-looking man. He was extremely large, for one thing, his formal white suit tailored exquisitely on a frame that didn't seem to hold a bit of fat. And he was, Michele thought, very old, even though his erect posture held the years at bay. He had a healthy thatch of snow-white hair, a full white beard, and dark eyes that shone benignly and contained a friendly, tolerant wisdom. Elegant hands were folded casually over the top of a gold-headed cane, which he used to lift aside the flap of the tent.

"Ladies." His deep voice was rich in tone and incongruously gentle for so large a man.

"How much?" Jackie demanded without preamble.

"You have a card?" he murmured. When she produced it, he added softly, "One free reading, then."

"Yours," Jackie told Michele, and pulled her friend inside.

Experienced in the various trappings of the fortune teller, Michele was surprised by the interior of the tent. There were no velvet hangings, no burning candles or incense, and no peculiar statuettes or symbols lying about. There was only a comfortable couch on one side of a low, plain, glass-topped table, with a chair on the other side. And bare tent walls.

The woman who rose from the chair at their

entrance was also something of a surprise to Michele. She was petite and delicate. Instead of the usual gypsy-type draperies she wore a very modern and tasteful ruby red dress that enormously flattered her snowy hair and milky complexion—to say nothing of a still-splendid figure.

"Welcome," she said softly, her voice low and sweet.

Jackie shoved Michele forward and waved her card. "My friend's come for her reading."

"Please sit down," Mrs. Fortune invited, seating herself gracefully in the chair.

Michele sat, with Jackie beside her, and watched as Mrs. Fortune leaned forward to open a carved wooden box at the side of the table. The woman seemed to hesitate only an instant, then drew out a deck of tarot cards wrapped in cloth. She unwrapped the cards and set the cloth aside, then held the deck out to Michele. "Cut the cards, please."

Obeying, Michele studied the woman curiously. She was absolutely lovely, her face totally unlined even though Michele felt she was very old. Her eyes were a vibrant green, so unusual a shade that they seemed iridescent, their depth and clarity curiously compelling.

Michele had a sudden and rather unnerving impression that if any mortal human had been granted the ability to open a door into the future, this woman had. She had remained purposefully silent and sat very still, all too aware that many so-called clairvoyants were adept at reading body language and listening to subtle changes in voice as they skillfully guided their "clients" through the practiced fakery of what was called in the craft of a professional seer a "cold reading."

But the beautiful old lady didn't even glance up, and she never once asked Michele anything. She laid the tarot cards out on the table slowly in a complicated pattern, studying each one in silence for an instant before placing the next. When the pattern lay complete, she began speaking in her soft, clear voice, her tone holding no drama or mystical theatrics. One delicate finger lightly touched each card as she interpreted it.

"Your past. You are descended from a very old line, their roots in the dark Celtic moors. In your veins runs the hot blood of a warrior strain, and in your soul is the knowledge of a terrible conflict you were born to resolve. An unexpected meeting cast all that you feel into chaos. There is a man you cannot trust, yet cannot turn away from."

Michele didn't stiffen, but only because she was concentrating fiercely on remaining motionless. Still, she could feel her pulse quicken, and the hands clasped together in her lap were cold.

The old lady went on without looking up. "Your present. You stand between enemies. Old, old enemies. All around you are the shifting patterns of things seen—and unseen. Events set in motion by your blood, but not by your hand. Old hurts must be avenged; the need for revenge is a terrible hunger, a dreadful thirst, and it must be satisfied. Danger is everywhere, a trusted voice, a strange but familiar face, eyes veiled against you. You feel great doubts and fears, but great passions as well. You risk much. Star-crossed lovers."

Michele heard Jackie gasp, but she herself remained utterly silent. She had a peculiarly detached feeling, staring at that delicate hand as it moved lightly from card to card, and listening to the soft, relentless voice.

"Your future. You will feel torn between what was and what must be. Two paths lay before you, one leading to the destruction of all you hold dear, the other leading to a triumph of the heart and the spirit. Neither way is without pain. Neither way is without tragedy. Even now, the events set in motion entangle you and all you care about; even now, the seeds sown decades ago grow twisted to bear a dark and bitter fruit. You cannot change what must be, but only preserve with your own will a hopeful future. The confusion of heart against mind is a battle you must fight and win if you are to find contentment. You must abandon much to win all. You must find courage in the truth you feel, for that alone will show you the way."

The old lady looked up then, her vibrant eyes darkened with compassion. Gently, she said, "It was always intended, child. Always meant to be. You were destined to love the enemy of your family."

Michele gazed into those sympathetic eyes, and she could almost feel them looking into her soul. "I don't believe in fate," she whispered.

"Yes, you do," Mrs. Fortune said quietly. "You've always known what he could be to you."

Michele didn't remember rising or turning away. She didn't remember walking from the tent. She just found herself outside, walking steadily beside a very silent Jackie, and when she heard her own voice shake she wasn't surprised. "Did you arrange that? Pay her to say that?"

"No." Jackie was too subdued to take offense. "If I had—she wouldn't have said what she did. The last thing I wanted to hear was that you were fated to love Ian Stuart."

"I don't believe in fate," Michele repeated.

"Are you in love with him? Michele? Are you?"

"Yes."

"That appears to have gone rather well," he said, coming into the tent.

She looked up from the cards still lying in their pattern on the table and stared at him. Her vibrant eyes held a speculative gleam. "Cy, what happened to the stacked deck?"

Mildly surprised, he said, "Wasn't it in the box?"

"No."

"Well, no matter, sweet. You were able to follow the script, after all."

"I wasn't following a script."

"No?"

"No. I read the cards just the way they fell. Each had only one possible interpretation."

He looked down at the pattern on the table, then back at her. In the depths of his benign eyes was a tiny smile. "Now, fancy that," he said placidly.

She shook her head slightly and leaned forward to gather up the cards. Conversationally, and as if to herself, she said, "I don't know why I'm surprised. After all these years, you'd think I would have become accustomed to it."

"To what, love?"

"Your witchery."

Cyrus Fortune folded both elegant hands on his cane and looked at her with a tender smile playing about his firm lips. In a sedate tone, he said, "She cut the deck. You dealt the cards and read them. How could I have possibly controlled that?"

A soft laugh escaped her, the sound tinged with love and wonder. "You didn't control it. You simply knew it would happen just that way." Then she sobered and looked up at him gravely. "Cy, if you had arrived on time thirty-five years ago . . ."

"Those two people would not now exist."

"Could you have ended it then?"

He hesitated. "There was a chance."

"I think you were right when you told me everything happens in its own time," she said. "And this is the time. They *were* meant to love."

"Yes."

"It isn't over, is it?"

"No," he said gently. "It's just beginning."


"Have you told him?" Jackie asked in a strained voice.

They were on the terrace of the hotel having a late lunch—or were supposed to be. Neither had done more than pick at her food, and both had been virtually silent until now.

Michele shook her head. "I want to. I've wanted to a dozen times. I just . . . somehow, I haven't been able to say the words."

"It was bad enough thinking you just had to have some insane fling. But this . . ."

"Don't you think I know?" Michele's voice was unsteady despite all her attempts at control. She looked at her friend, her emotions confused and uncertain. "Jackie, I didn't go looking for this. It scares the hell out of me, what Dad and Jon are going to do when they find out."

"Do they have to find out?"

"It isn't just an affair!"

Jackie looked away, finally, from her friend's glittering eyes. "All right. What does Ian say?"

"We've tried to talk about it. But there aren't any answers. No matter what we do, this is going to have a terrible effect on our families. The tension between them has never been stronger. Our fathers are competing for that big contract, both of them pushing to get their current projects finished. I don't know what's going on in Atlanta now, but Jon was convinced the Stuarts had paid off some of the inspectors, bribed them to stall the project."

"They've done it before," Jackie said flatly.

"Have they? That's the worst part of this feud, Jackie, and you're blind if you can't see it."

"What are you talking about?"

"Nothing's ever proven. Accusations on one side, denials on the other, over and over. But it's a *private* battle. Oh, half the South knows about it, but it's still private. We don't go to court, don't gather evidence to present to a jury. That isn't the way it's done. We just sling mud back and forth, and go on hating because it doesn't *end*."

Jackie was silent for a moment, then shook her head and met Michele's gaze with a stubborn glint in her own. "All I know is that you can't stop it. You heard what Mrs. Fortune said. Choose the wrong path, and you'll destroy everything you care about. And it doesn't take a clairvoyant to tell either of us that the wrong path is any kind of relationship with Ian Stuart."

Michele drew a short breath. "She also said I was destined to love him."

"She didn't say he was destined to love you."

That hurt, all the more because Michele felt so vulnerable and because the horrible, dark suspicions just wouldn't go away. There was a part of her that believed Ian cared about her, that it wasn't just passion, but so much had happened between them so quickly that she felt raw and unsure.

"Forbidden fruit," Jackie said in a taut voice. "Maybe he wanted a taste too."

"He wouldn't risk so much for that," Michele whispered. "Not simply that."

"What's he risking? His father wouldn't disown him," Jackie said, unknowingly echoing Ian's own words. "He's an only child, an only son. Besides that—maybe his father thinks that's all a Logan woman's good for. He might not give a damn that Ian's slept with you; it'd only give him something new to taunt your father with."

"Don't."

Jackie looked down, knowing Michele was on the ragged edge and hurting. "I don't want to keep saying such things. But you've got to face the fact that you're risking everything. Your father and Jon could never accept Ian as your lover. Never. Michele, they'd rather see you dead."

Michele got up from the table and walked away. She was moving blindly, hardly aware that she was retreating to her room like a wounded animal seeking its burrow. She desperately wanted Ian, wanted his arms around her and his body hard against hers. She wanted him to push away the darkness that seemed to be closing in on her, the confusion and pain.

Her friend's statement that both her father and brother would choose to see her dead rather than in the arms of the man she loved was a terrible thing to hear. But worse than hearing it was the devastation of believing it was true.

"Michele?"

"Leave me alone, Jackie." She was standing by her balcony doors, staring out.

"We can go home," Jackie's voice was pleading. "Today. Nobody has to know. Things can be the way they were—"

"Nothing can ever be the way it was." That was the only truth she was utterly certain of. Nothing in her life would ever again be as it had been.

"Look at what he's done to you already. You're so brittle, a touch would shatter you into a million pieces. This is tearing you apart. No matter what you do now it's only going to hurt you. Michele—"

Michele jerked around, but whatever she would have said was lost as the phone rang loudly. She drew a breath to steady herself, then went to the bed and sat down as she lifted the receiver. "Hello?"

"Michele."

She felt suddenly cold, a tremor of fear chasing down her spine. Her father never called her like this, not unless something had happened. "Dad? What's wrong?"

"Jon's been hurt." His voice was flat. "Early this morning at the building."

"How bad is it?" She was terrified of hearing the answer, more terrified of not hearing it.

"I don't know. They haven't been able to tell me anything definitive yet. He was barely conscious when they brought him in, but he managed to say who was responsible."

"Responsible?" The coldness spread through her body. "It wasn't an accident?"

"No, it damned well wasn't," her father said, his control slipping and allowing the harsh and malignant feelings he was experiencing to sound in his voice. "Jon caught a saboteur, Michele, red-handed. He managed to choke the truth out of him before the bastard's handiwork brought a wall down almost on top of him."

Michele couldn't have asked; she didn't want to hear. But her father was going on in a voice vibrating with hatred and filled with utter certainty.

"The son of a bitch thought he'd keep suspicion off himself by being out of the city when it happened, but his hired gun couldn't talk fast enough. Ian Stuart planned it all weeks ago, then called yesterday and set his man to work. If Jon hadn't gotten a tip and gone out there, the damage would have been ten times as bad."

"No." She thought she said it aloud, but her father apparently heard nothing.

"Come home, Michele."

"I'll be on the next plane," she murmured.

"The car will meet you."

Michele hung up the phone, vaguely surprised to see that her hand was steady. She felt hollow inside, all her emotions numbed and still.

"What's happened?" Jackie demanded anxiously. "You're white as a ghost."

Tonelessly, Michele repeated the conversation. "I have to go home," she finished.

"Start packing. I'll call the airline. And I'll pack too. I'm going back with you."

Michele didn't try to dissuade her friend. The next two hours passed in a blur, and it wasn't until they were on a plane bound for Atlanta that the numbness retreated and left her feeling emotionally battered and so confused she could barely think.

Ian? No! It couldn't have been him. It was all some horrible mistake; it had to be. There *had* to be another explanation for what had happened. He'd said he wouldn't fight her brother, that Jon could hate him to hell and back and he wouldn't fight him. Could he have lied about that and made her believe him? Could he have held her in his arms with a desire she knew was real while plotting coldly against her family?

She didn't want to believe it, *couldn't* believe it despite her father's certainty and her own agonizing doubts. How could she love a man capable of such treachery? There had to be another answer . . .

"Michele?" Jackie's voice was tentative. "You couldn't have known Ian would—"

"I don't know that he did."

"But your father said that man named Ian as his employer."

"Then it's his word against Ian's, isn't it?"

There was a moment of silence, and then Jackie said, "You must believe it. You didn't leave a message for Ian."

Michele kept her head turned away, directing her gaze out the window even though she saw nothing. "No, I didn't leave a message. I just ran like a coward. Afraid to face him."

"What could he have said if you had stayed to face him? That he didn't do it? Of course he'd say that. Michele, this time somebody got hurt. Jon got hurt. And Lord help the Stuarts if he was hurt badly."

"I know." Oh, yes, she knew. The fuse had been lit now, and it was only a matter of time before hate exploded. What had the fortune teller said? That the desire for revenge was a terrible hunger and thirst? Michele knew only too well that her father was hungering now, that whatever restraints had held the feud away from the brink of violence had been snapped. Her father wouldn't wait for proof; he had all he needed.

Michele stared out the plane window at the blanket of clouds below, fear for her brother and the painful uncertainties about Ian tearing at her, and filled with the knowledge that any hope of peacefully stopping the feud was gone now.

*"You cannot change what must be . . ."*

Was there nothing she could do except endure, stand by helplessly and watch while everyone she loved was torn apart by this?

The company limo was waiting when she and Jackie emerged from the frenetically busy terminal at the airport. Their luggage was quickly stowed, and they were driven directly to the hospital. It was still November in Atlanta, and far from paradise a cold rain was still falling. The city looked bleak and dreary, especially at night.

At the hospital, they were directed to the right floor, and as soon as they stepped out of the elevator Charles Logan strode toward them. He was still upright and vigorous in his sixties, conceding nothing to age except the gray streaking his brown hair and the lined, weathered face of a man who had worked much of his life outside. His gray eyes were the only similarity between him and his daughter; he was a tall man and powerfully built, his rugged features holding none of the delicacy Michele had inherited from their Celtic ancestors.

"Dad? Is Jon—?" She hurried toward him with Jackie at her heels.

"It's all right," he said, hugging her briefly. "A mild concussion and broken wrist, but he'll be able to go home tomorrow."

The relief was overwhelming, but Michele was still very aware of the tautness in her father's expression and the cold gray gleam in his eyes. "Can I see him?"

"Room 484. He's awake."

"I'll wait out here," Jackie said, obviously as relieved as her friend to hear the news.

With the somewhat courtly air he inevitably adopted whenever he was around young women —especially pretty ones—Charles Logan offered his arm to Jackie. "Why don't I buy you a cup of coffee?"

"Sounds good to me. Michele, tell Jon I said hi."

Nodding, Michele left her father and Jackie and made her way down the hall to Jon's room. She opened the door cautiously, but he was sitting up and looked around quickly, his frown smoothing away. There was a strip of bandage over his right eye, and his left arm was held in a cast from fingers to elbow.

"Michele! Sorry to drag you back from your vacation. Dad shouldn't have called you."

She crossed the room and bent over the bed to kiss him lightly. "Don't be stupid." She kept her voice easy with an effort as he smiled at her.

Jonathan Logan was a tall and physically powerful man like his father, and he shared the slightly rough-hewn features that made both men ruggedly good-looking. He had medium brown hair and had inherited blue eyes from both parental sides. But his father's genes were clearly strongest in him. Like the elder Logan, Jon was stubborn, a bit arrogant, and easy to anger. He was close to his sister despite a five-year difference in age, and his protectiveness of her stemmed both from his affection and from an extremely strong sense of family responsibility.

Michele had always adored her big brother, but love had never blinded her to his faults. He had never quite accepted the fact that she was a grown woman perfectly capable of taking care of herself; to

Jon, she was still the little sister with a troublesome streak of rebelliousness.

"You don't have much of a tan," he noted critically.

"I have enough. Haven't you been listening to the surgeon general?"

Jon grunted. "I've been listening to too damn many doctors in the last few hours. Pull that chair over and have a seat."

She obeyed, trying to keep her expression calm under his searching scrutiny. Apparently without success.

"You look worried to death," her brother said softly. "Cut it out. I'm fine."

Michele linked her fingers together in her lap and looked at them for a moment, then raised her gaze to his. "Jon, what happened?"

"I'm sure Dad told you."

"Yes. But I want to hear it from you."

He shrugged. "I got a tip yesterday afternoon—"

"From whom?"

"Beats me. A man, or sounded like it. Maybe one of Stuart's people turned traitor. He called the office and said if we didn't want anything to happen to the building we'd better keep an eye on it during the night."

Michele felt a helpless sense of anger sweep over her. "And, of course, you didn't even consider increasing security or calling the police."

Jon avoided her eyes. "I knew who it was, and I wanted to catch them at it. Hell, I'd been waiting for a chance like that for years."

"You could have been killed!"

"I wasn't." His mouth firmed stubbornly. "I decided not to tell Dad, to go myself. It seemed to me the only kind of sabotage the bastards could hope to get away with would have to be pretty subtle, but I knew they'd want it to be crippling as well. I rigged a couple of booby traps in the control room for the electrical system, figuring that was most likely. Then I decided to check the elevator banks, and that was where I caught him. He'd already planted explosive charges to snap the cables."

"What happened?" Michele asked, dry-mouthed.

"Well, I didn't know he'd set a timer that was busy ticking away. Once I got my hands on him, he was only too happy to talk. He said he'd been paid in cash—half up front a couple of weeks ago—and been told in detail what he was supposed to do. He'd gotten the call yesterday telling him to get busy. Ian Stuart hired him."

"He was sure of that?"

"Of course he was sure. For God's sake, Michele, he called him by name!"

Something was nagging at the back of Michele's mind, a lesson learned in her own investigative training. Slowly, she said, "Did he say how he was hired? I mean, had he met Ian Stuart in person, or was it some other arrangement?"

Jon was frowning at her. "I didn't have time to ask. The explosives went off, and instead of just snapping the cables, part of the blast went outward. Half a wall came down on top of me. I didn't know anything else until our security guys dug me out of there. Unfortunately, the saboteur was long gone by then, and we aren't likely to find him."

Michele looked at her brother searchingly. "But, don't you see, Jon? That man could have been hired to say anything. Maybe his job wasn't so much to cripple the building as it was to have the Logans and Stuarts at each other's throats. Maybe that's why you were tipped. Just so that you could be pointed at a specific target."

"What'd be the point?" But even as he asked, Jon was scowling.

"You know as well as I do. That Techtron contract is worth millions; the Logans and Stuarts are the top commercial builders in Atlanta, but not the only ones. If we eliminate each other, somebody else is going to come out on top. Look, everybody knows that Dad and Brandon Stuart are in a race to finish their current projects. Their bids on the Techtron contract were so close that the decisive question is: Who can start first? If both companies get bogged down in fighting each other, Techtron won't be able to start their project when they want—unless they hire someone else."

Jon shook his head. "The Stuarts are behind this, I know they are."

"Jon—"

"Dammit, Michele, they've already tried to sabotage us! They've bribed the inspectors to slow us down."

"How do you know that?"

"I told you. I have a source at city hall."

"How good a source?"

"He's never been wrong. And I pay him a fortune to make sure he never is."

"Maybe somebody else is paying him more."

Jon moved restlessly on the bed. "Will you listen to yourself for a minute? You've dreamed up this whole conspiracy theory just because you don't want to admit the Stuarts are out to get us. You've always given them the benefit of the doubt."

"What's wrong with that? Jon, you don't have

any proof. You've never had any proof—just reports from elusive sources that you pay to feed you information. Sources who could be taking somebody else's money to tell you what you want to hear. And I didn't *dream up* the fact that everyone in Atlanta knows the Logans and Stuarts would rather fight each other than anything else. You don't have to tell me the explosion wasn't reported to the police, or even to the insurance company; the feud doesn't work that way and everyone knows that too."

"So?"

"So, a third party could easily decide they could do what they liked without any threat of being caught or prosecuted. They could know that the Logans and Stuarts would never look further than each other for a villain. Just point us at each other and keep applying pressure until we destroy ourselves."

"That's ridiculous, Michele."

"Is it? Is it any more ridiculous than—than carrying on a battle that started with some petty grievance nobody can even remember more than five centuries ago? Any more ridiculous than hating because we're *supposed* to hate, because we've been told we should?"

"They're our enemies," Jon said, staring down at his immobilized wrist.

"Are they? Are you sure?"

"Yes. After—" He broke off abruptly.

"After what?" A memory surfaced, and she went on evenly. "Jon, you said something once about Brandon Stuart and Dad years ago. What happened then?"

"Never mind."

A wave of absolute fury swept over Michele, and her voice shook with it. "Never mind? That's a hell of a thing to say to me, Jon. You and Dad can't wait to launch an all-out war with the Stuarts, and you tell me to never mind? Don't you think it's my business? Damn you, it's my family too! I think I deserve to know why my father and brother hate so deeply they can't even be rational about it. Tell me!"

"All right," Jon snapped. He drew a breath, then said, "Thirty-five years ago, Dad and Stuart fell in love with the same woman."

Despite Ian's remark that the bitterness between their fathers must have been deepened by a woman, the information still came as a shock to Michele. "What?"

He laughed shortly. "Pretty, isn't it? Dad wouldn't say much, but she must have played them off against each other. Dad fell hard, would have done anything for her. And he thought she loved him when—well, when they slept together."

"What happened?"

Jon shrugged. "A few weeks later, she broke down and told Dad she'd made a mistake, that she had realized she loved Brandon Stuart. She and Stuart announced their engagement, and he was strutting like a rooster for having beaten Dad. I'm not sure what happened then, except that there was some kind of confrontation between them and the woman left. Just walked out on both of them, apparently."

Michele could see how her father would have been enraged at losing to a rival—pratically a Stuart—but the story seemed incomplete to her. There had to have been more to it than what Jon knew. "And that's why Dad hates Brandon Stuart so bitterly?"

"Isn't it enough? Dad loved that woman, Michele, and Stuart took her away from him."

Slowly, Michele said, "It sounds to me as if she made up her own mind, and probably with a lot of pain. But she ended up without either of them."

"Maybe she found out she didn't love Stuart as much as she thought. Dad sure as hell wouldn't have taken her back after that."

"Right." She stared at her brother. "Even though he loved her so much."

Jon's eyes narrowed at the sarcasm. "Obviously, you don't understand how Dad felt."

"Obviously. Has it occurred to you that Dad and Mom were married a little more than thirty-four years ago? His heart must not have been too broken. Or maybe Mom caught him on the rebound. Is that his story?"

"I didn't ask," Jon said tightly.

"Maybe you should. Maybe we should both ask." Michele wondered if she looked as shaken as she felt. How odd, to find that so many certainties in her life had been built on shifting sand. Her father had always talked as if his children's mother was the one great love of his life; now it seemed that he had loved once before, and that the emotion had been great enough to spawn an equally powerful hatred.

Holding her voice steady, she said, "That may or may not give Dad a good enough reason to hate. But what about us, Jon? Where is it written that we have to hate because of something that happened before we were born?"

"Michele, they're trying to ruin us!"

"And if they aren't?" Everything inside her seemed to be focused on her brother, all her will bent on finding a chink somewhere in the wall of hate. "If someone else is using the Stuarts—and us—for their own gain? Can you at least consider the possibility?"

"Give me some real proof," he returned flatly. "Something more than theory."

She rose to her feet and stood gazing down at him for a moment. "Isn't that funny," she murmured. "You didn't need any real proof to believe it was the Stuarts."

Jon didn't react or speak again until she reached the door. Then his question dropped quietly into the silence. "What's happened to you, Michele?"

She half turned to look back at him. "Maybe I don't want to be a lemming."

"A what?"

"A lemming. It's a little animal. Every so often, the lemmings crowd together and rush toward a cliff. They commit mass suicide. Maybe a few centuries ago, someone told them it was the right thing to do."

After a moment, Jon shifted his gaze back to his broken wrist. "See you at home tomorrow, Michele."

She left the room, feeling tired and angry. The anger was new, and she welcomed it, because it was better than pain and hopelessness. She was angry at the stubborn blindness of her father's and Jon's hatred, angry at whatever long-ago ancestor had started this mess, and angry at herself for not having the courage to tell Jon what had really happened to her.

As for the latter, she realized it was less a matter of courage than a desire to cause the least amount of pain by her confession. God knew this was the worst possible time to break the news to her family, though there would never be a "good" time. Still, if she could somehow stop the feud, or at least defuse it before something horrible happened, before someone else got hurt because of it . . .

She didn't get the chance to offer her theory to her father until late the following morning as he was preparing to go to the hospital and get Jon. The brunch they had shared had been silent, with Michele trying to think of the best way to bring up the subject and her father preoccupied with thoughts of his own. In the end, she blurted it out, and like Jon, her father didn't believe it for a moment.

"Don't be absurd, Michele. Jon choked a confession out of that saboteur."

"Maybe he was paid to lie."

"No, it was the Stuarts all right. And this time they've gone too far. Jon could have been killed, to say nothing of the time and cost to repair the damage to the building."

She felt cold as she looked into the hardness of her father's eyes. "What are you going to do?"

"Nothing for you to worry about," he said calmly.

"Not worry? Dad—"

The phone on the hall table rang just then, and her father grasped the interruption. "Get the phone, honey," he said, laying aside his newspaper and rising from the table. "If it's for me, tell them I'll be back in a couple of hours."

He went out into the hall with her to get his coat, and Michele answered the phone with half her mind still occupied with the possibilities her father was considering for revenge. None she could think of was at all comforting.

"Hello?"

"Michele."

Her heart seemed to stop and then begin pounding against her ribs. Nobody said her name the way he did, and just the sound of it made her ache with longing. But she couldn't talk to him, not now when everything was so confused, and not with her father three feet away shrugging into his coat.

In a polite voice, she said, "I'm sorry, you have the wrong number." And hung up the phone.

It was a pity, she thought vaguely, that phone manners didn't extend to the rest of life. If everyone apologized for the mistakes others made, the world might be a kinder place.

"Are you coming to the hospital with me?" her father asked briskly.

Michele stood in the entrance hall of their stately old home and looked at her father. "No. I haven't even unpacked yet. I'll see Jon later."

Looking at her narrowly, he said, "You're too pale. Did you sleep well?"

"Not very. Jet lag, I expect."

"Good thing you're still on vacation for the rest of the week. You should get some rest, honey."

"I will."

When she was alone, Michele admitted to herself that rest was the last thing she could afford. Unless she could somehow prove that neither Ian nor his father was working against her family—and prove it quickly—then violence from both sides wasn't just probable, it was inevitable.

As so often in the past, the calm but tense status quo between the families had been disturbed yet again. A rivalry that was equally matched and that employed the same tactics could hold steady for years with neither side gaining the upper hand; in world politics, it was called the balance of power, and though it was a brutally delicate highwire act, at least it preserved both sides. But it required no more than a single nudge to upset the balance.

And someone was supplying that push.

Michele wasn't even sure that her theory was correct. It was still possible that Ian's father was bent on delaying his rival's building. It was even possible that Ian himself had planned the sabotage. But she couldn't believe that. Despite all the doubts and dark suspicions, the almost instinctive compulsion to believe the worst of a Stuart, she simply could not accept that the man she loved was capable of such treachery.

She wanted desperately to see him, talk to him, but dared not risk that. Too many people knew of the feud, and both she and Ian were familiar faces in the Atlanta social and business worlds. If just one whisper reached her father's ears before she could defuse the situation between the families . . .

Michele squared her shoulders and went to get her purse and car keys. She was a trained investigator, and all her experience told her to start with the simplest question and work toward an answer. And she had her question.

Who would have the most to gain by setting the Logans and Stuarts at each other's throats?

# Six

Ian cradled the phone and sat gazing across his office. She couldn't believe he'd done it, he told himself, feeling the cold fear of his own answer. Not after all they'd shared. Even with twenty years of programming against anyone named Stuart, she couldn't really believe he was the kind of treacherous bastard someone had made him out to be.

Could she?

He wanted to call her back, to demand that she talk to him, see him. But he hesitated, because he knew what she was going through now, her brother injured in an "accident" that had Stuart written all over it and her father no doubt plotting to get even. And there had been no time for her to learn to trust him, no time for them to reach a real understanding of each other.

He had returned to the hotel, discovered she had left, and had nearly gone crazy in the hours it had taken him to get home and find out what had happened. His only consolation in those endless hours had been the certain knowledge that something *had* happened, that she wouldn't have run from him without a word otherwise. Even then, he had hoped it was something simple, something not touching on the feud.

A lost hope. It hadn't taken him long to find out what had happened, and he couldn't bring himself to blame Michele for refusing to talk to him; even if she wasn't sure he had caused her brother's injuries, the doubts had to be tearing her apart. Still, he had no intention of giving up. He didn't want to do anything to make the situation more difficult for her, and he was all too aware that this was not the moment to seek her out; one more spark between the families and Atlanta just might go up in flames for a second time.

"When did you get back?" his father asked, coming into the office.

"Late last night." Ian looked at him thoughtfully, unconsciously searching.

Brandon Stuart was so different physically from his son that he might have been forgiven a tinge of doubt concerning Ian's paternity, except for the fact that Ian was the image of a Stuart ancestor a few generations back. The elder Stuart had black hair distinguished by silver wings at his temples, dark blue eyes, and patrician features so fine they just missed being delicate. He was a couple of inches under six feet tall and slender.

A man who moved somewhat lazily, he tended to be calm, not given to outbursts of temper, his occasional anger usually taking the form of an icy rage as quiet as it was deadly. A reasonable man in most things, he'd been shaped by his heritage and his own experiences to regard the Logans with bitter loathing, but he hadn't gone overboard in his efforts to instill the same feelings in his son; though he had made his own feelings very clear without mincing words, the wife he had lost only a few years before had persuaded him that it would be wrong to teach Ian to hate.

He and his son shared a suite of offices on the top floor of a downtown building, a convenience since Ian was very much a part of the family business despite a growing list of clients he worked for independently. After his mother's death, the stately old home he shared with his father had proved to hold too many memories for them both, and they had decided to sell it. Ian had chosen an apartment near the office, while his father had moved into a condo farther out.

Close in many ways—and sharing similiar temperaments—their differing personal interests and frequent disputes virtually demanded that they lead separate personal lives. If too much of their time had been spent together, they doubtless would have been at loggerheads more often than not; living apart they managed a solid relationship built on mutual respect and an often rueful understanding of each other.

As Ian had told Michele, they continued to argue from time to time, and hotly, but since neither was willing to either force the issue or back down, their relationship was never pushed beyond the breaking point.

"Did you get the project?" Brandon Stuart asked now, making himself comfortable in the visitor's chair in front of the massive old pine desk.

"I got it. Howard wants the preliminary designs by the first of the year. He wants to start construction by spring."

Brandon nodded, then said, "You don't look too happy for a man who just acquired a lucrative client."

Flatly, Ian said, "Jon Logan was injured early yesterday morning at their building." He knew damned well that his father was aware of what had happened, and wasn't surprised by his mild reaction.

"Well, building sites are dangerous places. You'd think he'd know that at his age."

"It wasn't an accident."

Calmly, Brandon said, "Naturally, they blame it on us. Not surprising, really, since they haven't a hope in hell of completing their building on time now."

Ian drew in a sharp breath and released it angrily. "Just tell me one thing. Did you arrange it?"

"Of course not. Explosives? I hope I have better sense than to resort to that kind of violence."

"I hope so too."

Brandon studied his son and frowned. "You believe I'm capable of setting an explosion?"

"Where the Logans are concerned, I believe you're capable of almost anything. You didn't arrange it? You knew nothing about it?"

"I've answered both those questions." A shade of responsive anger colored Brandon's voice. "I certainly won't say I'm sorry for the Logans' misfortune, but I had nothing to do with it. What the hell are you so angry about, Ian?"

Until that moment, Ian had been half certain that his father had stepped over the line and resorted to violence. But he believed the denial—and it opened up a new and unsettling possibility. If not his father, then who?

After a moment, he said, "I managed to get hold of one of their security people early this morning. He didn't want to talk to me, but I finally convinced him there was no harm in just telling me what had happened. He was one of the men who helped dig Jon out after the explosion."

"So? What did he have to say?"

"Jon caught the saboteur red-handed. And the man told him that *I* had hired him to do the job."

"That's ridiculous," Brandon scoffed. "You weren't even in the country."

Ian shook his head. "You're missing the point, Dad. If that's what the man said, then the chances are good it's what he honestly believed. My guess is that he was paid to say I was responsible. Somebody set me up."

"For God's sake, Ian, all you know is what Jon said. Of course he'd pin the blame on you. It's just the excuse they've been looking for to turn this into a war."

Trying to hold on to his patience, Ian said, "Has it occurred to you that someone else could be taking advantage of the suspicion between the two families? That the objective wasn't to slow the Logans down but to start us fighting each other so that neither building is finished on time?"

"That's insane."

"And a five-hundred-year-old feud isn't?"

Brandon was silent for a moment, then shrugged. "Even supposing there's something in this idea of yours, what the hell do you want me to do about it?"

Ian knew the question was rhetorical, but he chose to take it literally. "I want you to do nothing to aggravate the situation until I can find out what's going on."

"If you think Charles and Jon Logan are going to sit still after this, you're mistaken. They'll strike out at us, Ian, and I won't sit still for that."

For the first time, Ian began to understand how a feud could continue for centuries. It was a blind, automatic response: you hit me and I hit back. Toss hate and suspicion into the equation and it became a never-ending circle.

"Dad, somebody has to stop this insanity."

"You think you can?" his father asked dryly.

"I'm damned well going to try. I'm sick and tired of the whole mess. But it won't do me much good to try and find answers unless you agree to back off."

Brandon studied him for a moment, then shrugged. "I'll increase security around the building so they can't get near it, and I'll keep my mouth shut for the time being. But that's all I can promise, Ian. If this thing gets even uglier, I'm not about to sit still for it."

Ian knew his father too well to ask for more. He was reasonably sure the Logans wouldn't move immediately to exact revenge, since plans take time. At best, he'd have a little breathing space, but not much. A few days, maybe a couple of weeks.

The first thing he had to do was reach Michele. He wanted to see her so badly that it was a constant, dull ache inside him, and the possibility that she could believe he had arranged the sabotage tore at him. Intellectually, he knew that things had happened too fast between them, that with the best will in the world Michele couldn't overcome twenty years of brainwashing in only a few short days; emotionally, he wanted her to believe in him, to trust him no matter what her family said.

Another impossible hope.

He had known that what he felt for Michele was more than passion, more than desire, but some barrier in his mind had refused to let him see the truth of his own feelings. Whether, as Michele had lightly said, it was stamped in the genes or merely in the mind, a tradition of hatred and mistrust spanning centuries was a difficult thing to surmount. Desire he could admit, but love had quite literally been unthinkable.

Until it had happened.


Michele came into the house a bit warily. She'd been gone all day, first to the building site where Jon had been hurt and then to her office. The company she worked for had always been tolerant of their investigative staff's erratic work hours, and no one had been much surprised to see her appear with days still left of her vacation. She had shut herself in her office and spent hours working by phone and by computer, trying to find some proof that a third party was intent on causing friction between her family and Ian's.

The results had been nebulous, leaving her feeling frustrated and worried.

"Michele."

She looked up to see Jon coming down the stairs toward her, his broken wrist in a sling. He was frowning, and she felt sorry the moment she realized her extended absence had worried him. She put her purse and car keys on the hall table and waited for him.

"Shouldn't you be in bed?" she asked lightly. "Where's Dad?"

"No, I'm fine. And Dad's in his study working on the books. Where've you been?"

She managed a smile. "Jon, when are you going to realize that I'm not a kid anymore?"

He reached the bottom of the stairs and stood looking at her, his eyes narrowed. "I asked a simple question, Michele. Would it hurt you to answer?"

Well, she'd expected it. "I suppose not. I went down to the building. I wanted to get a look at the damage and see if I could find any part of the timer left intact."

"You shouldn't have gone down there." His frown deepened, and he added unwillingly, "Find anything?"

"Bits and pieces." She knew that Jon respected her training and abilities as an investigator, even though he had never agreed with her choice of career. He didn't like the idea of his sister poking around the burned-out remains of buildings in cases where her employers suspected arson, or dealing with people unscrupulous enough to try other ways of bilking insurance companies.

"You can't do much with that."

"I've worked with less."

"Okay, I'll bite. What did you figure out from the bits and pieces?"

His mocking tone sparked Michele's temper. She crossed her arms over her breasts and spoke deliberately. "Well, I figured out that the device our saboteur used didn't come from around here. It's state of the art, and right now you can only find it on the West Coast—if your connections are good enough, and you're prepared to pay through the nose."

"So? It's the jet age."

"True, and therefore I did some checking. The Stuarts haven't had anything shipped in from the West Coast for more than three years, their jet hasn't been west of the Rockies in nine months, and no employee has been out of Georgia at all this year."

Jon was honestly startled. "How in God's name did you find all that out?"

"It's what I'm trained to do. I piece together puzzles, Jon, and since insurance companies work with the police sometimes, I have access to a lot of computer data banks."

He scowled. "Then you missed something. One of them called and ordered the device, or went after it and used a commercial flight."

"No calls to the West Coast, on their business or private lines, in the last year. And neither of them has been out there on any commercial flight this year."

"Then they hired somebody to get it!"

Michele drew a breath. "Why would they? Why be devious on that end and then hire an explosives man who knew exactly who he was working for? It doesn't make any sense. And another thing, Jon, who tipped you?"

"What?"

"Somebody called and told you to keep an eye on the building; who was it?"

"How the hell should I know?"

"Didn't you even stop to wonder? Didn't it bother you just a little bit that for the first time in my knowledge you were tipped hours ahead of time that something was likely to happen?"

"Maybe one of their employees got cold feet."

"Know your enemies; after five centuries, we certainly do. We don't involve employees in the feud;

neither do they. In fact, it's strangely out of character for them to hire an explosives man."

After a moment, Jon turned and went into the living room. Michele, feeling the first glimmer of hope that she was getting through to him, followed and sat on the arm of an overstuffed chair near the door. She watched as he went behind the bar in one corner, waited patiently while he fixed himself a soft drink.

"I could use something stronger," he muttered, "but the doctor said not to for a few days."

"Jon, don't you see that the sabotage at the building just doesn't fit the Stuarts'—or our—way of fighting? Sure, our families killed each other right and left at first, but there hasn't been a death or serious injury caused by the feud on either side for more than a hundred years. And no open destruction, not like that, not something that could easily get the police involved. There aren't any duels anymore, or outright murders. We fight in other ways now. Subtle, sneaky ways, unethical certainly, and sometimes illegal, but not violent."

He was staring down at his drink and looked up only after a long silence. His gaze was searching, his expression seemed troubled and faintly anxious, maybe even wary. When he spoke his voice was matter-of-fact. "All right. I'll do some checking myself. If there's somebody else in this, they have to be after the Techtron project, like you said. The number of builders who could handle the work is limited; I should know something within a few days."

Michele almost held her breath. "And Dad? Can you keep him from doing something crazy?"

"I'll try."

She nodded, weak with relief. "Good. Maybe one of us can find some proof."

"Misha?" Jon was looking at his glass again. "What did happen to you?"

Not for the first time, Michele acknowledged that her brother read her face and her moods too well; he knew that this intense and stubborn defense of the Stuarts was new, that it had to have been caused by powerful events or feelings. Maybe he even felt the change in her, or saw some sign of it. She wondered if she looked different but didn't ask him that. And she didn't tell him the truth, because he was still unconvinced and she dared not risk an admission that would both shock and enrage him.

"I told you," she said finally, steadily. "I don't want to be a lemming. Five hundred years is five centuries too long to hate."

Jon might have probed deeper, but the phone out in the hall rang just then and Michele welcomed the interruption. "I'll get it," she told him.

He nodded, still looking at his glass.

She went out into the hall and picked up the receiver. "Hello?"

"Michele. Don't hang up."

Driven by urgent necessity, she had managed to keep her thoughts off Ian, but now the sound of his voice, the way he said her name, was like the shattering of a dam holding back floodwaters. The feelings swept over her so powerfully that she could only endure them in silence, her eyes closing as she fought the urge to blurt out her love and pain and fear.

"Michele? Dammit, talk to me!"

She opened her eyes and glanced toward the living room, very aware of the quietness in the house and her brother's keen hearing. In a voice that was little more than a whisper, she said, "I can't. Not now."

"Baby, I didn't do it. I swear to God I didn't."

She swallowed hard. "I know."

"I have to see you," Ian said intensely.

"It isn't possible."

"We can meet somewhere. Now, tonight."

"I can't."

He hesitated, then said in a flat tone, "Then I'll walk up to your front door and ring the bell."

It might have been an empty threat; Michele thought it probably was, because he knew the risks as well as she did. But the fact that he made it at all told her something of Ian's state of mind. She tried to weigh the risks in her own mind, but all she could think of was how badly she wanted to see him. Needed to see him.

"All right," she murmured. "Where?"

"Three-twenty-four South Highland. I'll meet you in the lobby." He hung up.

Michele cradled the receiver and stared down at it for a moment. After checking Ian's phone bills, she knew that address; it was his apartment building. She took a deep breath, then went to the living room doorway and spoke casually to her brother.

"I have to go out for a while. Tell Dad and Leona I probably won't be back for supper." Leona was their housekeeper.

"Where are you going?" he asked immediately.

"You worry too much, Jon. See you later." Before he could demand an answer, she quickly retreated to gather her purse and keys, then left the house. She wasted no time in driving her Cougar away from the neighborhood; it was doubtful her brother would resort to following her, but she was already taking one chance too many.

The evening traffic was fairly light, and she pulled into the parking lot at the apartment building just over half an hour later. Since it was well past dark, the building showed few features except for lighted windows stretching upward, seemingly into infinity. Michele parked her car and made her way to the entrance; it was a security building, so the bright lobby boasted a guard at a high desk who looked up as she came in.

Then she saw Ian walking toward her. She hadn't seen him in more than twenty-four hours, and it felt like forever. He was wearing dark slacks and a white shirt open at the throat with the sleeves rolled up over his forearms, and she wondered vaguely how she could have seen him across crowded rooms for years without realizing that he moved like a big cat, with riveting grace and power.

Or maybe she had realized. Maybe she had known it for all those years, without being able to admit it to herself. Maybe that was why no other man had ever stirred her blood.

His eyes were darkened, his face very still. He took her hand without a word and led her toward the elevators. The guard, unsurprised and uninterested, went back to his magazine.

Neither of them spoke in the elevator. Michele looked down at their entwined hands, and for the first time a sense of peace and certainty stole over her. The fortune teller's warning flitted through her mind, and she knew that, right or wrong, she had chosen the path she had to follow.

The elevator opened onto the top floor of the building, and Ian led her down the hall to his door.

The moment they were inside, he pulled her into his arms and held her tightly.

"You didn't believe it," he said huskily. "Thank God you didn't believe it."

"When I left Martinique, I wasn't sure," she admitted, holding on to him fiercely. "Dad was so certain. But all the way back here I kept thinking that you *couldn't* have, that it simply wasn't possible."

Ian drew back just far enough to kiss her. "After you hung up on me this morning, I was afraid you believed it," he murmured against her mouth.

Michele smiled up at him as he lifted his head. "Dad was in the room," she said simply.

His eyes burned down at her. "I know we need to talk," he said in a hoarse, thickened voice, "but right now all I want to do is carry you to bed."

The rough statement made Michele's legs go weak, and her heart begin to pound erratically. Heat blossomed inside her. She shrugged off her shoulder bag, letting it drop carelessly to the floor, and lifted her arms to encircle his neck. "Please," she whispered.

Ian groaned as he gathered her up into his arms and strode through the apartment to his bedroom. What she did to him! From the first time they'd made love Michele had been completely uninhibited, so utterly honest and natural in her desire that it had stolen his breath. It was nothing short of miraculous that she could feel so strongly for him of all men; and the knowledge that she had never felt it for another man made it even more astonishing. It was as if all the fiery passion inside her had lain dormant waiting for him.

He set her on her feet beside his bed and turned on the lamp on the nightstand before sweeping the covers impatiently away. Then his fingers went to her neat braid and unclipped the narrow barrette; her thick hair freed itself instantly, unwinding from the severe style until it tumbled about her shoulders in a dark, shining cloud. He loved the look and feel of her hair loose, loved to run his fingers through the long, silky curls.

She was coping familiarly with the buttons of his shirt, pulling the tail free of his pants, and as she pushed the material off his shoulders he shrugged free of it.

"Wait," he murmured, catching her hands as she reached for the buckle of his belt.

Michele was no longer even mildly shocked at her own fervent eagerness. "Why?" she whispered.

Ian kissed her hungrily, then eased down on the edge of the bed and drew her forward to stand between his thighs. "Let me," he said huskily, slowly unbuttoning her silk blouse.

She caught her breath and went still, watching his absorbed expression. She understood dimly that Ian wanted to make it last, and fought to control her own wild need. His deliberation fed the exquisite tension spreading all through her body, and she could feel her heart thudding unevenly.

He reached the final button and slowly pushed the blouse off her shoulders, his hands lingering to stroke her arms lightly. Michele shivered and forced herself to remain still, even though every instinct urged her to move. He unfastened her slacks and pushed them down, and this time she moved only to step out of her shoes and nudge them and the pants aside.

Ian found the front clasp of her bra and opened it, but instead of stripping the flimsy cups of lace and satin away he bent his head forward to nuzzle between them. Michele felt his warm lips, the gliding touch of his tongue between her breasts, and her hands lifted to stroke his thick hair unsteadily as all her senses responded wildly to the caress. She could hardly breathe, and bit her bottom lip to hold back the sounds rising inside her.

He held both his hands at her narrow waist and used his lips and tongue to push aside very slowly the material hiding her breasts from him. When the straps slipped off her shoulders, she shrugged the bra to the floor, her fingers returning immediately to twine in his hair. For long moments he concentrated on the flushed and swollen curves, his mouth tasting her firm flesh with scalding hunger. Michele couldn't be still now, because her breasts were full and hot, the nipples so tight they were actually painful. Her fingers dug into his thick hair, and a moan escaped her throat.

"Ian, please," she whispered, sure she wouldn't be able to bear the sweet torture a second longer. The tension inside her was so great it was as if she hung suspended, anticipation coiling like agony. And then his mouth closed over a taut nipple, and she jerked at the instant, fiery pleasure, crying out because there was no room inside her to contain the incredible sensation. All the remaining strength flowed out of her legs, and she almost collapsed against him.

His hands slid over her bottom and lifted her, and she instinctively parted her legs as he settled her onto his lap. Only his pants and her silken panties separated them, and she was desperate to feel his flesh against her, and inside her. His mouth on her felt wonderful, but she wanted more. When his lips finally trailed up her throat to find hers, she kissed him wildly, demanding that he stop the torment.

A chuckle or a growl rumbled in Ian's chest, and he rose still holding her tightly against him. He turned and bent forward to lay her on the bed, then straightened and swiftly got rid of his remaining clothing. He couldn't take his eyes off her as she lay waiting for him. He had never really noticed what desire looked like on a woman's face, but on Michele's it was something he couldn't get enough of. Her delicate beauty altered with passion, grew somehow more intense, and he thought he had never seen anything more lovely. Her haunting eyes were pools of smoky gray, infinitely deep, a siren's eyes filled with eons of secret female wisdom, and in her husky voice was the ancient enchantment that could steal a man's soul and make it her own.

He came down on the bed beside her and covered her mouth with his, as frantic with need as she was. He hadn't wanted to hurry, very conscious of the fact that it could well be some time before they would be able to meet again, but both his urgent desire and her inflaming response were snapping the threads of his control. He was past the point of being able to move slowly; his craving for her was a compulsion that couldn't be mastered.

He stripped off her panties roughly and then spread her legs and moved between them. The need to bury himself in her, to sheathe his aching flesh in her welcoming heat was overwhelming, but a deeper, more powerful need kept him braced above her just on the point of entry.

"Michele," he said in a voice he hardly recognized, a voice that was strained and guttural because it came from a place inside him almost too profound for words. "Michele, I love you."

She was utterly still for an instant, staring up at him with wide, bottomless eyes. Then those eyes were filled with emotions so stark he almost wanted to hide his own eyes from them, almost wanted to look away and tell her not to feel that much for him because he couldn't bear it. But he had to bear it; he had no choice. What he felt for her was just as primitive, every bit as complex and wonderful and terrifying as what he could see shining in her eyes.

She lifted her head to kiss him, and a smile of wonder curved her lips as her arms tightened around his neck. "I love you," she whispered. "I think I've loved you all my life. Ian . . ."

He groaned, a wild tangle of love and desire coiling inside him until he thought he'd burst with it. Slowly, he bore down until the tight heat of her body enclosed him. He wanted to fill her with himself, to fuse them together in flesh just as this essential love was fusing them in spirit.

Michele had thought she could never feel more than she had on Martinique, but she was wrong. With love acknowledged on both sides, it seemed that some final, dimly perceived barrier between them had shattered. Every physical sensation was more intense, the intimacy more stark, the joining more complete. The emotions inside her surged until they couldn't be contained, until they escaped in tears and broken murmurs of love.

Passion had formed the first tenuous bond between them, but it was love that anchored and strengthened it, love that reached across a chasm left by five centuries of hate. A strong, solid bridge was built out of the most fragile and powerful emotion of the human heart, an emotion that was all the more remarkable because it existed between two people who were born and bred to be enemies.

In the lamplight quiet of the bedroom they lay close together, both still caught up in the wonder of their own feelings. Ian was the first to speak, his voice low and husky.

"No going back."

Michele lifted her head from its resting place on his shoulder and looked at him gravely. "Was there ever a point when we could have?"

He brushed a strand of her silky black hair away from her cheek, his hand lingering to stroke her soft skin. "I don't think so, baby. Even with everything against us, we fell in love. Maybe we never had a choice."

After a moment, Michele told him about her visit with Jackie to the fortune teller, repeating as much of the prediction as she could remember. "I've never believed in that," she finished. "Fate. But now I can't help wondering. She couldn't have *known*, Ian, not so . . . so completely. She said I was born to resolve an old conflict, and destined to love the enemy of my family."

Ian didn't scoff, even though he was a man with little faith in so-called psychic abilities. With a slightly twisted smile, he said, "I'd like to believe it was just a fluke, but if I were truly master of my own fate, I would have kept driving when I saw you by the roadside."

"You didn't know it was me," she objected.

His smile deepened. "Oh, yes, I did."

"But you looked surprised when I turned around."

Ian raised his head and kissed her, then admitted, "I was surprised. Shocked, really. I didn't understand what I was feeling until later; all I knew was that I took one look at you and knew you could never be an enemy."

Her smile faded. "I'm sorry I left the island without a word. I was just so confused."

"I know. And worried about Jon. The hospital said he had a slight concussion and a broken wrist. How is he?"

"He's up and around." Michele frowned. "I think. . . . He acts as if he believes I'm different somehow. I've been trying to make him at least accept the possibility that somebody else is behind the sabotage, and he's suspicious of my motives."

"You think he might guess about us?"

"I just don't know. And I don't know how he'll react if he does guess. A week ago I would have said he'd go after you with a gun, but . . ."

"But?"

"It's a feeling more than anything I can put my finger on. He seems. . . . It's as if he's fighting to hold on to the hate even though the emotion's just half there."

"Habit, maybe." Ian looked thoughtful.

Michele wished she could focus on whatever it was she sensed about Jon, but shrugged it away for the moment. "Anyway, I spent the day trying to get some evidence he'd accept, and I finally convinced him to at least check a few things himself."

After a moment, Ian said, "We really do have to talk about this." Even as he said it, he was stroking her slender body gently, unable to stop touching her. "Why don't we have a shower and then go rustle something up in the kitchen?"

"Can you cook?"

"Yes. Can you?"

She smiled gently. "No."

"Trouble boiling water?"

"Oh, I can do that."

"Then you can make the coffee."

Michele did make the coffee, but only after a prolonged interval in Ian's shower. And it was while they were digging into the excellent omelettes he had prepared that she made a somewhat rueful statement.

"I think I'd better get a prescription for the pill."

With an answering smile, Ian said, "Maybe you'd better. I can't seem to be practical when I get near you."

Michele had done a bit of calculating after coming home from Martinique, and she had a strong feeling that unless either she or Ian were infertile she had very likely already conceived. Her cycle was extremely regular, never influenced by stress or emotion, and her next period was due in less than two weeks. Her doctor would doubtless want to make certain before putting her on any form of birth control.

The timing, of course, was hardly perfect, but Michele couldn't find it in herself to be disturbed. If she was carrying Ian's child it would delight her; even now, just the possibility sent a surge of utter contentment through her. She wanted a baby, their baby, and no doubts or shadows over the future could dispel that longing.

"What are you thinking?" he asked suddenly, huskily. "Your face is so soft." It was more than that, but he couldn't find the words to explain what he saw. Just as passion made her fiercely beautiful, this mood now made her lovely in a new and strangely moving way. She looked serene, mysterious, the little smile curving her lips both tremulous and pleased.

Meeting his intent gaze, she said softly, "I'm thinking that I might be pregnant. There's a good chance."

Ian felt his throat tighten as he reached across the small table and took her hand. The thought of his child growing inside her delicate body made him realize just how badly he wanted it to happen. For the first time, he wondered if his carelessness had been, on some deep level, deliberate. "I know we haven't found all the answers yet, but no matter what happens I'm not going to lose you. Marry me."

Michele didn't think about how their families would react or about anything else except the happiness filling her. Nothing in her life had felt as certain as this. "Yes," she whispered.

Some time later, with no clear idea of how she'd gotten there, Michele sat up to find herself on Ian's lap; they were in the living room, and he was sitting on the couch. She had no fault to find with the arrangement, but a glance at his watch made her say in surprise, "I've been here for hours."

Ian looked at the watch as well and sighed. "Dammit, I don't want you to leave."

In spite of her happiness, the reminder made her aware of all the problems lying ahead of them. "I don't want to go. But we have to be careful, Ian. You know that."

"I wish it were a joke," he said broodingly. "The Hatfields and the McCoys. A comic strip in the Sunday paper. But even when our feud was comical, it wasn't very funny. And it isn't funny now. We're forced to act like teenagers with disapproving parents, as if we aren't mature enough to make up our own minds. I don't want stolen meetings and phone calls on the sly, Michele."

"Neither do I." She swallowed hard, then added steadily, "We have to stop the feud—or at least prove somebody else is involved it in."

"And if we can't?"

She drew a deep breath and met his eyes gravely. "Ian, I'll marry you tomorrow if you want me to. I'll live with you here or anywhere. No matter what happens between our families, I want to spend the rest of my life with you. But I'd always blame myself if I didn't at least *try* not to hurt Dad and Jon."

"I know." He kissed her gently, then forced himself to concentrate. "You said you'd spent the day trying to find evidence. Any luck?"

Michele told him what she'd found out about the explosive device the saboteur had used. "It isn't much, but it is something. That timer came from the West Coast, probably from California. And it wasn't cheap."

Ian was frowning. "Odd. If somebody's trying to push the feud toward violence, why use a device that neither side could easily acquire? A bundle of dynamite or a lump of plastique would have done the job just as well, and both are easily available in construction work."

"I know, that's bothering me, too. If the purpose was to cover his—or her, I suppose—tracks, it would have been smarter to go with the ordinary. Something as uncommon as that device could be traced back to a buyer."

"Do you think you can do that? Trace it back?"

Michele hesitated. "Maybe. Given enough time. And the odds are better if it was purchased legitimately. The company I work for has a West Coast office, and I have a contact there who owes me a favor. He might be able to find something."

Ian nodded slowly. "You work on that end, and I'll see what I can find out here in Atlanta. If one of our rivals is behind this, somebody knows about it; you can't keep such an elaborate plan completely quiet."

"It's going to take time," Michele reminded him. "And that's something we don't have a lot of. Jon promised to try and keep Dad from retaliating, but I don't know how long he'll be able to." She paused, then said quietly, "We can't do anything that might strike a spark. In the state he's in, it won't take much to push Dad over the edge."

# Seven

Ian was silent for a long moment, then sighed roughly. "I know what you're saying. As much as I hate to admit it, I even agree. But I don't know how long I can stand not seeing you, Michele."

She felt the same; the thought of not seeing him, possibly for weeks, made her ache inside, but she concentrated on the belief that maybe—just maybe—they could find a way to keep from building their future on the ruins of their families.

"It won't be easy," she admitted. "And even if we do find proof that someone else is involved, we might not be able to stop the feud. But we have to try, Ian. I don't think either of us could be happy if we didn't at least try. If just one person—the wrong person—sees us together. . . . Too many people know about the feud. Too many people who don't understand how serious it is. The whole thing could blow up in our faces. We can't take the chance."

He pulled her against his chest and just held her for a long moment, his cheek pressed to her silky black hair. "All right," he said quietly.

Michele wanted to stay in his arms forever, and even though she knew she should leave she couldn't make herself go. "What will your father do when he finds out about us?"

"I honestly don't know. He won't like it, but whether he'll accept it is something else. He's willing to concede the possibility of a third party being involved in the feud—especially now that he knows neither of us caused that explosion. And he doesn't like being used; that's to our benefit. I'll keep trying to convince him."

She half nodded. "If I can get Jon on our side, maybe he can help me convince Dad." Then she sighed and gently pushed herself upright again. "I'd better go; it's almost midnight."

Ian didn't protest again, even though he wanted to. She certainly knew her father better than he did, and if she believed he was so close to the edge, then they had to avoid calling attention to their relationship, at least until they could somehow manage to defuse the tension.

He walked her down to her car, reluctant to let her go until he absolutely had to. Standing by her Cougar in the brightly lit parking lot, he pulled her into his arms and kissed her, wishing they had another hour, another night. It was so bitterly unfair that the woman he loved, the woman who might well be carrying his child even now, couldn't walk beside him in public for fear of violence exploding between their families.

"I love you," he murmured against her lips, holding her tightly. "No matter what happens, don't forget that."

"I won't forget. I love you, too. And I'll fight for us, Ian, I promise you. I don't want to destroy my family, but if I have to make a choice—"

"You won't," he interrupted firmly, even though he knew it could easily come to that.

Insistently, she said, "If I do, I'll walk away from *them*—not you."

He held her for a moment longer, then reluctantly let her go. "I hope you don't have to." He reached into his pocket and withdrew a key, pressing it into her hand. "A key to the apartment, just in case. I'll tell the security guard he's to let you pass at any time."

"For when Dad throws me out?" she asked in a light voice that didn't quite mask the pain.

Ian touched her cheek gently. "Any time. We don't know what could happen, baby. If you need to come to me, for any reason, then I want you to."

"All right."

Another worry was nagging at him, and as she got into the car, he added, "Michele, . . . be careful. Both our families have an enemy now, and he doesn't seem to care who gets hurt."

The caution sent a chill through her. She hadn't thought about it that way, but the ruthlessness of an enemy who could plant explosives and then lure a potential victim to the site—even if the intention was merely to point suspicion at someone else—was only too obvious.

*Neither way is without tragedy.* The fortune teller's warning crept into her mind, and she shivered. "If I find out anything, I'll call you."

"Call me anyway," he said. "If I don't at least hear your voice, I think I'll go out of my mind." He made no pretense of keeping the statement light; his voice was low and rough with unhidden feeling.

Michele nodded, her throat too tight to speak, and when he closed the car door she started the engine and backed out of the parking space. He remained there, gazing after her, and her last glimpse of him in the rearview mirror showed her only a big, shadowy figure with gleaming hair under the stark lights.

She drove home slowly, trying to think, to plan. Even with the damage to her father's building, he was only weeks away from completing the project, just as Brandon Stuart was weeks away from finishing his building; both had been originally scheduled to be completed by the first of the year, and that deadline was a critical one if either company hoped to win the Techtron project. The race was still on, more intense than before, and if the saboteur meant to cause more trouble, he was likely to find plenty of opportunity. He would probably wait at least a while, hoping that he had done enough to start the centuries-old hatred boiling, but if neither side reacted, he'd have to throw more wood on the fire. Logically, he would strike at the Stuarts next, a seeming retaliation from the Logans, assuming that Michele's father didn't strike first.

How much time did they have? Very little, she knew. And unless she could convince Jon the Stuarts weren't behind the sabotage, there was no hope at all of controlling their father. He might listen to Jon, even if he didn't like what he heard, but he wouldn't listen to her.

She parked her car in the curving drive of their big, old house and let herself in quietly. There was a lamp burning in the entrance hall, but the rest of the house appeared dark. Leaving her purse and keys on the hall table, Michele started up the stairs. She was on the third step when Jon's voice came quietly from the dark living room.

"A little late, aren't you?"

Michele waited there as he slowly crossed the hall to the bottom of the stairs and stood looking up at her. She felt a flash of resentment, but it quickly vanished; she couldn't afford the emotion, couldn't take the chance of alienating Jon over his usual protectiveness.

Dryly, she said, "I talked Dad out of the curfew when I was twenty, remember? This isn't the first time I've come in after midnight."

"No," he agreed. "It's usually your job, at least according to you. But you're on vacation this week, Michele." His gaze was very intent, searching; she had the feeling that he wanted to ask her outright where she'd been, but that for some reason he didn't want to hear the answer.

Because he thought he knew the answer.

Michele wondered if it showed on her face. Keeping her voice calm, she said, "Yes, I'm on vacation. I'm also trying very hard to find out who ordered the sabotage. Your source at city hall, Jon—I want to talk to him."

The distraction worked, at least for the moment.

"He's on vacation," Jon said. "Up north somewhere."

"Now, isn't that . . . convenient," she mused, more to herself than to Jon.

"For God's sake, Michele, he takes a vacation every year!"

She looked at her brother. "In November?"

Jon hesitated, then swore softly. "No. Usually in August. And, before you ask, I don't know if he took his regular vacation this year; I had no reason to be in touch with him that month."

"Did he tell you he was going on vacation?"

Again, Jon hesitated. "No. I have his home number, and I called his house tonight. His wife answered and said she was packing to join him."

"For how long?"

"Couple of weeks, maybe more."

Even granting her suspicions where Jon's informant was concerned, it still sounded to her as if the man had left Atlanta in something of a hurry. She didn't like it. She didn't like it at all.

"Misha. . . ."

"Maybe I can track him down," she said, saying the first thing that came into her head. Because Jon had been about to ask her a question she wasn't yet ready to answer; she'd heard it in his voice.

"He could lose his job if you start asking questions about him."

She wasn't at all sure she cared; paid informers weren't her favorite people. "I'll be discreet. But I'm going to find out who's behind this, Jon. You could have been killed, and Lord only knows what could happen next." The very thought of what could happen next, all the myriad possibilities woven like a net around the people she loved, made her feel cold and afraid.

After a long moment, Jon said, "You're very sure someone else is involved."

Michele drew a deep breath. "Positive. I'll need your source's name and anything else you know about him. We'll talk in the morning."

"All right. Good night, Michele."

"Good night." She went on up the stairs to her bedroom on the second floor. And it wasn't until she was changing for bed that a glimpse in the bathroom mirror told her what Jon had seen. It wasn't in her face or eyes; the light in the hall downstairs hadn't been good enough for that. But it had been good enough for him to see a definite change. When she'd left the house hours before, her hair had been neatly braided in its accustomed style. She had forgotten to put it back up before leaving Ian's apartment; it now hung loosely around her shoulders, the curls a little wilder than usual because she'd gotten her hair wet in the shower.

Michele couldn't think of a single good reason why she would have taken her hair down—except the truth. And she didn't think Jon had been able to think of one either. Sooner or later, he'd ask the question, and she'd have to answer.

Sooner or later.

The following days passed slowly. Michele got in touch with her counterpart on the West Coast and persuaded him to try and find out who had acquired the state-of-the-art timer.

"Legally, or under the table?" he asked, frankly curious since she'd told him the matter was personal rather than business.

"Both, if you can manage it; I have no way of knowing if he had a legitimate reason for buying the thing. I can't even tell you how far back to look, Steve. At a guess, a few months. There are only three legitimate sources on the West Coast, and the thing's so new there *can't* be many illegitimate ones. But this guy may have really covered his tracks."

"So you want a list of every buyer for, say, the last six months? That's a tall order, Michele."

"I know. But if you come through for me, I'll owe you a dozen favors."

"Um. And I suppose you need to know yesterday?"

"Yesterday wouldn't have been soon enough."

"Gotcha. Okay, I'll see what I can do. I know of a few shady dealers in explosives, so I'll try them too. I'll let you know as soon as I find out anything."

"Thanks, Steve."

"No problem. By the way, are you as gorgeous as you sound?" He always asked that, and Michele always gave him the same calm answer.

"No. I have crossed eyes and buck teeth. If you can't reach me at the office, call me at home." She recited the number.

"One of these days," he said pleasantly, "I'm going to fly east and find out for myself."

"Don't bother."

"Ah—she has a man in her life."

Michele could hardly help but laugh. "Yes. And, believe me, that's a story in itself." The thought of Ian made her recall the saboteur's apparent motives, and she added more soberly, "Steve, along with that list of names—see if you can get descriptions of the buyers, okay?"

"Descriptions? Why?"

"He might be using an alias. I'm groping in the dark; he's nameless and faceless."

"Michele, you want to tell me what's going on?"

She had never met Steve Ashe, but over the past couple of years they had talked frequently, and phone relationships between strangers were sometimes close simply because they were unlikely to meet face to face. The normal guards of people came down somehow, until a name and a familiar voice became a friend.

"... *a trusted voice, a strange but familiar face, eyes veiled against you.*"

She shivered unconsciously as the fortune teller's warning flitted through her mind. Stupid to bank too much on that, she told herself. There was no way to look at cards on a table and see into the future, just no way. But her uneasiness grew. So much of the reading had been uncannily on target.

"Michele?"

"Sorry. My mind wandered for a minute."

"Are you going to tell me?"

"There isn't much to tell. A project of my father's was sabotaged, and I need to find out who's responsible."

"The police can't help?"

"No." She didn't elaborate.

Steve sighed. "When I call in my favors, one of them's going to be a request to hear the whole story."

"Find out who bought that timer and I'll tell you gladly."

"Do my best. I'll be in touch, Michele."

After she'd hung up, Michele sat at the desk in her office for a long time thinking. There were innumerable details she could check, nebulous though they were. The rival companies here in Atlanta that could handle a project the size of the Techtron contract numbered only a half dozen or so; she could begin looking into them, searching for the signs of equipment, supplies, and manpower being readied for a big project and, conversely, those same resources being already committed to an on-going project and unavailable for anything new. She could piece together the recent histories of the owners of those companies and look for ambition and/or a driving need for a lucrative contract.

Jon had promised to do some checking on his own, but Michele had no intention of leaving it entirely up to him. He knew the construction business better than she did, but she had the training and experience in gathering evidence piece by piece and putting it together.

Assuming she was given the time.

She was grateful to have the work to do, not because it took her mind off all the problems—it could hardly do that—but because she felt less helpless with a definite plan of action, however sketchy. And if she was never distracted from her longing to be with Ian, at least working herself to the point of exhaustion allowed her to sleep at night.

Two weeks passed, with no results on either her end or his and no chance for them to safely meet, and Michele was very conscious of the growing tension in them both. She could hear it in Ian's voice when they talked briefly on the phone, and she felt it in herself. And it wasn't just one kind of tension, because they couldn't be together; they were edgy waiting for their saboteur to make his next move, frustrated by their inability to find answers, and very conscious that time was running out.

The only bright spot during those weeks was Michele's inner certainty that she was indeed pregnant. She almost held her breath when her period was late, but by the fourth day she was sure. She called her doctor—from the office, of course—and made an appointment after briefly discussing the matter with him and settling on a date that would ensure the test was accurate. She decided not to mention it to Ian until it was confirmed, but she was certain.

It was a bittersweet joy. She felt all the wonder and happiness of a woman who wanted her baby with all her heart, and yet she couldn't forget the presence of a nameless, faceless enemy who could destroy everyone she loved—possibly even her unborn child. Ian had promised to be careful, and so had Jon, but Michele's anxiety wasn't eased.

And when the answers finally did begin falling into place, they brought only a new set of questions.

Steve came through with flying colors, even though it took him nearly three weeks to cover the necessary area on the West Coast. He sent the list directly to Michele's computer, and it was obvious he'd done a thorough job. As soon as she looked over the information, she called him.

"I owe you a dozen favors," she said.

"And I'll make you pay through the nose." Then he sobered. "Any help at all?"

She studied the list on her computer screen. "I'm not sure yet. You've got about thirty names here, and all but three of them are located on the West Coast *and* legitimately involved with demolitions work. No addresses on these three?"

"No, sorry. The names are probably aliases; all three bought a timer from a man who had no business selling them, and all three paid in cash; it's a miracle he got names from them. I got descriptions of two: George Norris is a blonde in his twenties and looked mad as hell at somebody, and Robert Andrews is dark, slick, and probably a thief of some kind. The opinions are those of the man who sold the timer."

Michele looked at the third name on the list. "And Nicholas South?"

"Now, there," Steve said with satisfaction, "we hit a wall. Our shady dealer in rare explosives just couldn't seem to recall what Mr. South looked like. In fact, he had all the signs of having been paid to keep his mouth shut. Would your man be cagey enough to buy a little silence?"

"He might," Michele said slowly, feeling the first flicker of real hope. "Steve, do you think that dealer would be willing to talk if the price were right?"

"I think he'd sell his soul for the right price. How high do you want to go?"

"As high as it takes. Just get the information and I'll wire you the money."

"It may take a few days or more," Steve warned. "The guy operates out of a van, and he doesn't park in one place for very long."

"Let me know as soon as you find out something."

"Right."

Michele didn't know if a description of the elusive Mr. South would do her any good at all, but, like Steve, she was doubly suspicious of anyone who paid to cover his tracks. As for the companies and men she was checking here in Atlanta, four rival construction firms had been eliminated with fair certainty; all four were currently involved in lengthy projects demanding all their resources and couldn't possibly have taken on the Techtron contract. She had two companies left to check; if those proved doubtful as well, then she'd have to try and discover another motive for the sabotage.

As the days turned into weeks, his simmering rage began to boil. All the careful planning, the moves timed and executed with the precision of chess pieces on a board, had not produced the results he'd expected.

Something was wrong. They weren't reacting as they should have done. By now, the fight should have been fully begun. They should have been tearing each other to shreds while he enjoyed the sight from the sidelines. Instead, the tense balance had somehow been maintained, with both families quiet.

He thought about it for a long time, struggling to contain his rage so that he could consider. He knew, of course, about the curious twist of fate that had entered his game; that knowledge was certainly a weapon he could use to his advantage. But he had decided to time that perfectly, to choose just the right moment to strike the final destructive blow.

Still, he had the uneasy feeling that someone else was using the very knowledge he meant as a weapon somehow to heal the damage he had already inflicted. Not them, no. They couldn't possibly have overcome what he'd done to them; there was no way she'd trust him after he had hurt her brother. And they hadn't seen each other, he knew that.

But he was disturbed. His plan had been meticulously arranged, yet now he could feel an alien touch, a ghostly hand deflecting or softening his blows. The conduits through which he had so carefully fed information were being severed before they could be used to further antagonize, the buffers between himself and his enemies moved silently out of the way. He was less protected now.

He looked down at the devices on the table, and his control over rage slipped another notch. So be it, then, he decided angrily. He would have to be bolder, strike with less concern of protecting himself. Another push, and if they failed to react, follow that with a deadly shove.

It occurred to him that deaths would bring the police into the situation, but he was beyond caring. No one would look further than the feud for suspects. There had been no fatalities in more than a hundred years; perhaps it was time to teach them a forgotten lesson about the power of hate.

Like the month before, December bowed with a cold rain designed to make warm-blooded Southerners shiver miserably. With the Christmas shopping season in full swing, the city was gaily decorated, but the bright splashes of color, vibrant lights, and glittering tinsel did little to cheer gloomy skies.

Michele, who usually scorned anything but a light jacket in winter, dug her fur coat out of the closet whenever she left for work each morning. Her workload was unusually light for this time of year, so she was able to devote most of her time to the painfully slow search for an enemy.

She had done her best to track down Jon's informant, but that gentleman had either hidden—or been hidden—very thoroughly, and she had no luck. As for the rest, she spent long hours sifting through information, frustrated by the elusive feeling that she was looking in the wrong place entirely, that there was something she was missing.

"Michele?"

She looked up from the papers spread out on her desk to find her brother standing in the doorway. It was late Friday afternoon, the leaden skies and bitter cold outside promising sleet or freezing rain within hours.

"Has something happened?" she asked instantly, her heart leaping into her throat.

"No, not that I know of." He came into the office and sat down in the chair in front of her desk, looking as tired and tense as she felt. He'd been unusually quiet these last weeks, almost subdued, watching her from time to time with an expression she couldn't define. He had managed to keep their father from retaliating against the Stuarts, though not without a struggle; Michele had overheard at least one bitter exchange between them and knew that the two of them were at odds for the first time she could remember.

Jon was becoming convinced despite himself. He had quietly agreed with Michele when she eliminated four of their rivals, and had offered the reluctant opinion that the remaining two firms were already stretched too thin to be able to take on the Techtron project.

"What are you doing here?" she asked finally, gathering the papers into a neat stack and tucking them into a folder.

"I came to take you home."

"Jon—"

"Look, you've barely come up for air in weeks. You drag home at eight or nine o'clock at night, and you head back here before this place is even open for business. The security guard downstairs told me they've been letting you in and out because you're the first one here and the last to leave. You can't keep up this pace, Michele. You've lost weight, and you look so brittle I'd be afraid to touch you."

Jon wasn't the first to scold her, although her doctor had been even more blunt about the matter. She'd lost eight pounds he didn't think she could spare, and even though that happened sometimes early in a pregnancy, he told her she had to start taking better care of herself. Especially now.

Michele had made an effort after the doctor's warning, forcing herself to eat and to get enough sleep, but she hadn't been able to slow down because what she was doing was so terribly important to her. With every day that passed, she was more and more conscious of time ticking away. Something was going to happen; she could feel it like a cold, dank fog, like something that could be seen and felt but not captured.

She set the file aside and shrugged as she gave in to her brother, feeling the tension in her shoulders and neck. "All right, all right. I'll go home."

"Good," he said. "You can get some rest before the party."

Blinking, she said, "What party?"

Patiently, he said, "Look at your calender. It's that annual charity do to raise money for the disadvantaged kids in the city. Christmas, remember? It's just around the corner. You go with me every year, and I bought our tickets a couple of months ago."

"I really don't think—"

"It'll do you good to get out. Jackie'll be there. Come on, Michele."

It was a black-tie event, the first of the glittering

social functions scheduled between now and New Year's, and Michele had attended most of them in the past. On the point of trying to get out of it this year, she suddenly remembered that Ian always went; she'd seen him across the ballroom.

Did Jon know that? Gazing at her brother's veiled eyes, she had the uneasy feeling that he did. It would be insane for her to think she could be in the same room with Ian—even a crowded ballroom—without giving her feelings away. And she hadn't yet told him about the baby, wanting to be with him for that, to see his face when he heard; how could she stay away from him when the longing to be in his arms tortured her?

"Come on, Michele," Jon repeated. "You promised, and I'm holding you to it."

"Is Dad going?" she asked slowly.

"No. He said he had things to do."

It was madness, but she wasn't surprised to hear herself give in. "All right."

Jon's eyes flickered, but that was his only reaction. He rose to his feet. "Get your coat, and I'll walk you to the car."

Michele didn't argue. Even with herself.

A few hours later, she stood before the dressing mirror in her bedroom, fastening her earrings. A long, hot bath had eased some of her physical tension, but she knew she was still edgy. She had tried to disguise at least the outward indications of that, applying makeup to soften her face and shade her eyes, and wearing a gown that was made up of flowing lines and soft material.

She wore her hair in a style less severe than usual; it was piled high on her head in a mass of loose curls, with a number of long curling strands allowed to trail over one shoulder. The gown she wore was a shimmering gray; long-sleeved and with a deep V neckline, it had a full skirt falling from a high waist.

She'd been too busy to pay much attention to her own appearance these last weeks, and for the first time, she could see the signs of strain in herself. With no excess weight to spare, the lost pounds had left her obviously thinner, but despite that she looked neither ill nor exhausted. Her eyes seemed larger, her cheekbones more prominent, but it was a finely honed look as if some drastic alteration had taken place inside her, leaving her starkly different and yet curiously more focused, more centered than she had been before.

It was too early in her pregnancy for that to cause such outward changes, but Michele thought the child she carried was at least partly responsible nonetheless—because of her emotional awareness. There was a bond between her and Ian now that could never be broken no matter what happened. Their love had created a new life, a tiny scrap of humanity both Logan and Stuart. The bridge they had sought to build between their families had become in part a living connection.

Michele held on to that awareness, because it gave her strength. She went to her closet and got the cloak Jackie had talked her into buying back in the fall. The long, hooded cloak was pale blue and trimmed in ermine; it was both exotic and dramatic, and Michele hadn't yet worn it because she hadn't been able to get up the nerve. Tonight she swung it around her shoulders automatically with no more than a faint inner shrug and went downstairs.

Jon didn't say very much during the drive downtown to the hotel where the event was being held, but he did tell her something that made her believe he was well on his way to being convinced someone other than a Stuart was working against them.

"I played a little hardball with one of the electrical inspectors this morning."

Michele looked at him, worried. "What did you do?"

Jon smiled thinly. "Since we weren't having any luck finding my guy at city hall, I went straight to the horse's mouth. I took with me half a dozen signed statements from other builders who are positive he took bribes to delay their projects. They didn't have proof, mind you, but he knew damned well the statements alone would get him fired."

"He talked?"

"He sure did. He admitted he'd been paid to delay us. The arrangements were made by phone, and he was paid in cash, by messenger; half up front and half a week after our crews were forced to stop working. His employer didn't identify himself, but from what was said, he gathered the man was a Stuart."

"It wasn't," Michele said flatly.

"No," Jon said just as flatly, "I don't think it was."

"Why?" she asked.

"Because the inspector had a lot more to say. And he was surprised I didn't know." Jon snorted almost angrily. "Serves me right for being so damned convinced the Stuarts were behind it that I never looked for anything else."

"Tell me."

"He said there had been a lot of quiet talk these last weeks about somebody working against us and the Stuarts. Apparently, it's all over the grapevine: inspectors, suppliers, even the crews on both jobs. A hell of a lot of money's been paid in bribes and kickbacks, but nobody knows who's behind it. The thing is, it's as if this guy has inside information; he seems to know exactly when and where to cause delays that cost both us and the Stuarts in time and money."

"You think he's buying the information?"

"He's bought everything else." Jon sounded frustrated. He was handling the car easily despite the cast on his left arm, and scowling through the windshield.

After a moment, Michele said, "Have you told Dad?"

"I've tried. He doesn't believe it, Misha. He's convinced the Stuarts are behind everything. I've been able to hold him back only because both projects have been stalled. But I don't know how much longer I can manage it."

There was little she could say to that, but something else was nagging at her. "Jon, you said a lot of money had been spent in bribes and kickbacks. How much?"

"Can't know for sure. Tens of thousands. Maybe even hundreds of thousands."

Recalling all the data she'd collected on the last two possible rivals, Michele said, "That's too much. None of our rivals could spread that much money around even if they wanted to; all their capital's tied up, and their personal fortunes just wouldn't cover it."

"Then who the hell's after us?"

"I don't know. But we have to find out."

The remainder of the drive was silent. Michele tried to think of an answer, but all she had were questions. If not a business rival, then *who*? If not for the gain of the Techtron project, then *why*?


Ian had almost decided to skip the charity event. He was hardly in the mood to make polite social chit-chat even for a good cause. He was here because he had suddenly remembered that Michele had attended last year.

The hardest thing he'd ever done was to stay away from her after they had agreed it was best. The brief daily phone calls had done nothing except heighten his desire to see her, to be with her, until he felt frustration gnawing at him. Simply not seeing her was bad enough; the knowledge that someone was intent on playing very nasty games with both families made him worry constantly about her safety. He wanted her with him, wanted her close, so that he could watch over her.

If anything happened to Michele, Ian knew he'd lose his mind. It was an icy fear that never left him now. He had never felt that kind of fear before, but he knew that it would always be with him, for as long as he lived. Because he loved Michele, he would never shake the terror of losing her.

But that was a fear that came from love, a natural result of giving a hostage to fortune. It was the other pressures that were so rawly painful. The pressures that came from a feud neither of them wanted any part of. He knew it was madness to come here tonight hoping to at least see her across a crowded room, because it would only be a glimpse that would torment rather than satisfy. And that aching knowledge made him all the more determined to stop the damnable feud.

The bitter legacy of his family's hate was this— that he was forced to steal glances at the woman he loved.

He saw her when she came in with her brother. He had positioned himself across the huge room at an angle where he could best watch the entrance. There was quite a crowd, and because this was a buffet dinner, most of the people were on their feet and moving around. A pianist in the far corner played music that was no more than unlistened-to background noise.

The instant he saw Michele, Ian forgot about giving himself away to anyone who could be watching. He couldn't take his eyes off her. She was wearing a gleaming gown the exact shade of her gray eyes, and as she moved into the room beside her tall brother she looked beautiful and delicate—and changed.

She had lost a little weight, and that made her appear almost fragile. Yet there was something about her that was stronger as well, an elusive intensity as if all the force of will that made Michele uniquely herself had been compressed and focused inside her. Rather than breaking from the stresses all around her, she had grown stronger and surer. Like a diamond, Ian thought, a thing of incredible beauty and unmatched strength born under unimaginable pressures.

He watched as she and her brother were joined

by the red-headed Jackie and a tall, dark man who was apparently her date. It was almost impossible for him to think about anything except Michele, but gradually he became conscious of something nagging at him. There was a wrongness somewhere, something he saw or didn't see, and it disturbed him.

"Ian's here," Jackie said in a low voice, after pulling Michele from the group that had gradually formed around them. Jon and Cole Sutton were talking with a man about computers, and neither seemed to notice their dates moving away.

"I know." Michele hadn't dared search the room for him, but she knew he was here because she felt it.

Jackie stared at her, lips compressed. "It's still going on, isn't it? You and him."

Michele had avoided her friend since they'd returned from Martinique, partly because she'd been working so hard and partly because of Jackie's feelings about Ian. Now, steadily, she said, "I love him. And he loves me. Is that so hard for you to believe?"

"The explosion—"

"Ian wasn't responsible for that. And neither was his father. There's somebody else, Jackie, somebody who wants to destroy both families."

"That's insane."

"Yes, it is. But true. Even Jon can see that now."

Jackie was frowning, but her expression cleared as Cole Sutton slipped away from the group around Jon and joined them. "Did you sell him a computer?" she asked, slipping her arm familiarly through his.

"No luck. He's the old-fashioned kind." Cole was a tall, dark man somewhere in his thirties with a face so handsome his features were almost delicate. He had deep blue eyes and a slow smile, and he reminded Michele of someone although she hadn't been able to decide who it was. He was a sales representative for a high-tech company that had a flourishing office in Atlanta, and like many salesmen he was a charming man with an easy manner.

Jackie had been seeing him for only a few months, but she had fallen quickly and hard. Having finally met the man, Michele could see why, but he made her just a little uncomfortable. Something about the way he stood beside Jackie gave Michele the impression that he was hardly conscious of her, and that was definitely odd considering that they were lovers.

"Better luck next time," Jackie sympathized, smiling up at him with unshadowed love.

Cole didn't appear to notice that look, since he was glancing around the room absently—but someone else did. Michele saw her brother coming toward them, and in the few seconds that Jon's eyes rested on Jackie's face, his feelings were as plain as neon.

*He's in love with her.*

For the first time, Michele understood why her undoubtedly handsome brother dated rarely and tended to throw himself into his work. Jackie had never shown the slightest romantic interest in Jon, treating him with casual friendliness and nothing more; she had even confided in him about her romantic problems with other men. And now she was glowingly in love with Cole, totally unconscious of Jon except as Michele's brother.

Michele felt a pang of compassion and wondered why she had been so blind to his feelings before this.

"I'm ready to eat," Jon said calmly as he joined them. "How about the rest of you?"

There was nothing Michele could say to help him, so she said nothing. They went to the buffet together and then found a table, all four of them talking casually. The noise level in the room increased, and Michele could feel her tension increase as well until she could hardly stand it. She excused herself softly and left the table, but instead of going to the restroom she retrieved her cloak from the attendant and slipped out a side door that led to the rooftop terrace.

In good weather, the glass doors of the ballroom were left open so that guests could wander out onto the terrace. The frigid weather tonight made that impractical, so the doors had remained closed and the lights on the terrace hadn't been turned on. Michele had been here more than once, and knew her way despite the darkness. She avoided the light spilling out from the ballroom as she made her way to the far corner of the terrace and stood looking out on the lights of the city.

It was bitterly cold, but the sleet had held off and there was no wind. Even high above the city, the air was still, the traffic noises from below only muted sounds.

Michele waited. And when he came to her, she turned instantly to burrow into his arms. "I couldn't stand it anymore," she whispered, all her senses flaring almost painfully at the touch of him against her.

"I know. I couldn't either." Ian turned her face up and kissed her, the first gentleness deepening rapidly to become intense hunger. He held her slender body tightly, knowing that this was the danger they'd faced by staying away from each other; the very passion that had drawn them together in the face of a centuries-old feud was literally too powerful to be denied, and the long separation had built pressure in them both like steam under a tightly closed lid.

It didn't matter that more than a hundred people laughed and talked only a few yards away, many of whom would have been shocked to see a Logan and a Stuart in each other's arms. All the reason and common sense and caution in the world couldn't lessen their response to each other.

# Eight

"Michele. God, I've missed you." Ian raised his head at last, staring down at her, realizing with a jolt that it would be years before he knew her face the way he needed to; every time he looked at her she was new and different and more lovely. Now, in the faint lights of the city all around them, she was almost unreal, like something he had dreamed out of the night.

She laughed shakily, clinging to him. "I've missed you, too. I knew it was crazy to come here tonight, but I had to see you, even if it was just for a little while—"

Ian kissed her again, trying to satisfy the craving inside him and knowing it was impossible. "A little while isn't enough," he said huskily. "Michele—"

He broke off abruptly as she stiffened in his arms. Even though the light was too faint for him to see it, he knew she had gone pale. Keeping one arm around her, he turned slowly and saw a tall figure moving toward them across the terrace. All his instincts told him who it was, and even though the light from the ballroom was behind Jon and left his features in shadow, Ian could feel himself tense warily.

"Ian." There was no expression in the even voice, no hint of emotion or reaction of any kind. It was the first time he had spoken to Ian in their adult lives.

"Jon." It was a peculiar feeling, Ian thought, a sense of knowledge without familiarity, of caution and understanding, affinity and distance. They had been set apart all their lives by the feud, but now the woman both of them loved was a connection between them.

Michele's brother came toward them until he was only a few feet away, then stopped. Still without inflection, he said, "They're paging you in the ballroom. An emergency call."

The apparent calm of Jon's reaction hadn't eased Ian's wariness, but he felt some of Michele's stiffness drain away as if something in her brother's voice had lessened her own fears. She looked up at him, clearly more worried by the message than by the messenger.

"Something's happened?"

"I left this number with the security service at the building," Ian told her.

"I'll wait here," she said. When he hesitated, she added quietly, "It's all right."

Ian knew from Michele's reports that her brother had been looking for evidence just as they were, but she hadn't been sure that he believed both families had a common enemy, which made Jon's calm now hardly reassuring. Still, Ian had to trust Michele's assessment, and he couldn't believe her brother had any violent intentions.

Not, at least, at the moment.

"I'll be back," he told her, reluctantly leaving her to cross the terrace. As he came abreast of the other man, he hesitated, then said, "I'd never hurt her, Jon."

After a moment, Jon's only response was, "Better take your call."

Ian glanced back at Michele, standing so quiet and still, then swore under his breath and left them alone.

When he had gone, Michele watched her brother cross the remaining few feet between them and stand by the low terrace wall gazing out on the city. Having been braced for a thunderclap, this mild reaction made her more than a little wary, but she wondered now if the combination of Jon's growing belief in their faceless enemy and his seemingly hopeless love for Jackie had made him examine his own feelings. All she knew for certain was that he hadn't been surprised to find her out here with Ian.

"Cold place for a tryst," he said finally in the same expressionless tone.

It was cold, but Michele was only now aware of it. She drew her cloak more closely around her. "Not a tryst. It wasn't planned. None of it was planned." Her voice was as quiet as his, almost hushed, as if they were both afraid of disturbing some fine, delicate balance of emotion.

He drew a short breath. "I think I always knew it would happen someday. From the time you were about fourteen, and your favorite story was *Romeo and Juliet*."

"I'd forgotten that."

"Had you?"

"Consciously, yes. I loved that story. But I hated the ending. People shouldn't have to die for love, Jon. And they shouldn't have to hurt their families *because* they love."

After a moment, still without looking at her, Jon said, "When you came back from Martinique, I knew you were different. Then the day I got out of the hospital, you went out, and when you came home, I knew there was a man. I couldn't even accept the possibility that it was Ian Stuart, but you were fighting so hard to prove they weren't our enemies, and I couldn't get that out of my mind. I—finally called your hotel in Martinique to find out if he'd been registered there."

"When did you call?"

"A week ago."

He had known that long and had said nothing. She had done her brother an injustice in believing he'd react instantly and with hate, Michele realized. It seemed that Jon had given this a great deal of thought before facing his sister.

"Dad doesn't know." It wasn't a question.

"He isn't ready to hear that. I don't know if he ever will be, Michele."

She stepped close to him. "And what about you? How do you feel about it?"

An odd little laugh escaped Jon, a sound that wasn't amusement. "Hell, I don't know. I thought I hated him. But I came out here expecting to find you two together . . . and I didn't feel much of anything. I wanted to be suspicious of his motives, but I saw the way he looked at you. And the way you looked at him."

"We didn't want to hurt anyone. That's why we've stayed away from each other. We want to prove to Dad and Ian's father that someone else is working against the families, and stop the feud now before someone really gets hurt." Michele hesitated, then added quietly, "We're going to be married, Jon."

Without surprise, her brother said, "Dad can't stop you. But he won't accept it."

"Will you?"

Jon turned to look at her for the first time. "I have to, don't I? You wouldn't have gone this far without really thinking it through, not knowing all the risks you're taking. There's nothing I could say to you that you haven't already said to yourself. It can't have been easy for you. If you . . . love him after everything you've heard for twenty years, then it must be a pretty strong love."

"It is. The strongest, surest thing I've ever felt."

He half nodded. "That's why I have to accept it. Maybe Dad can cut off his nose to spite his face, but I can't. You're my sister, Michele. I just want you to be happy."

Though she was still afraid of her father's reaction, Jon's acceptance lifted at least part of her dread. "I was so afraid you'd hate me," she said unsteadily.

He smiled crookedly. "No. Right now, I'm finding it a little hard to hate anyone. I've decided I don't much fancy being a lemming. You were right about that. Five centuries is too long to hate."

"Good," Ian said in a quiet voice as he rejoined them. "We can use your help. Our not-so-friendly bomber has struck again."

Michele half turned to him, instinctively reaching out until his long fingers closed over hers. "Not your building?"

"The elevators. All of them except one; apparently, the man was scared off by security before he could finish the job. The guards saw someone disappear into the stairwell, then everything hit the fan and they were too busy to chase him."

"Was anyone hurt?" Michele asked anxiously.

"No. But I'd like to know how in hell he got into the building."

She looked at her brother. "It wasn't Dad, was it?"

Jon shook his head immediately. "No. He gave me his word he wouldn't retaliate without telling me, and he doesn't break his word."

Accepting that, Michele looked back at Ian and told him what Jon had found out from the bribed inspector. He heard her out in silence, then said, "If that many people know someone else is involved, one of them may know something that can help us. I'll start questioning our men in the morning."

"I'll do the same," Jon said. "And our suppliers."

Looking at Michele, Ian said reluctantly, "I have to get to the building. Dad was notified right after I was, so he'll be there. I have to talk to him."

"Will he listen?"

"He'll listen." Ian sounded grim. "I'm not going to give him a choice about it."

"I'll wait for you inside, Michele," Jon said, leaving them alone on the terrace.

After a moment, Ian pulled her into his arms and held her tightly. "Was he being tactful? Or does it test his resolution to see us together?"

A bit wryly, she said, "Maybe a bit of both. It wasn't easy for him; I think he's a little numb. But at least he's on our side now."

Ian kissed her. "I'm glad—for all our sakes, but

especially for yours. I know how much it would have hurt you if he hadn't been able to accept this."

Hugging as much of him as she could, Michele said fiercely, "I just wish it were *over*. I don't want to be afraid that something terrible's going to happen. I want to be with you. I love you so much . . ."

"I love you, too, baby," he murmured.

The endearment brought vividly to mind what she wanted to tell him, but there just wasn't time. It wasn't something meant to be related during a brief phone call or hurriedly in a stolen meeting on a cold terrace.

She drew away slowly. "You'd better go. I'll call you tomorrow."

Ian framed her face in his hands and kissed her, then again because it wasn't enough, it could never be enough between them. "Be careful," he warned tautly. "Whoever he is, this enemy's too bomb-happy for my peace of mind."

Michele nodded and watched as he crossed the terrace and went inside. For the first time, she felt very, very cold. And very much alone.


He had watched and listened from the deepest shadows of the terrace, his bitter rage growing. Damn them! They'd made peace among them, forming a solid union despite the odds and a lingering wariness between the men. He should have destroyed the love affair at the first sign, he realized, shattered it before bonds of trust could be formed. Now the three members of the younger generation had formed an alliance, all working to neutralize his attempts to disrupt the careful balance between their families.

And even worse. They knew about him. It was

only a matter of time before they put all the pieces together and discovered who their common enemy was.

For an instant, as the woman stood alone near the edge of the terrace, he was tempted to leap across the darkness separating them and push her over. Just a quick shove, and she'd fall to her death. Problem at least partially solved.

But he resisted the hot impulse, watching with glittering eyes as she went slowly back inside. He had to get them all, the three of them. And he had to do it in such a way that their fathers would be utterly convinced who was guilty.

That, he thought with satisfaction, would certainly push them both over the brink of sanity. Their children engulfed by the feud, neither of them would stop until one or both of them was dead. With a little luck—it would be both.

The plan began forming rapidly in his feverish mind. They thought the feud should end—so did he. But he wanted a swifter, cleaner death than the whimpering peace they sought. He intended for the pure white flame of revenge to annihilate all the dark, twisted remnants of hate.

Even the ones inside himself.

He had to do it. They'd given him no choice. He had to burn away the darkness before it consumed him.


Ian looked at the damage, thinking that even if the security guards had failed to capture the culprit, at least they'd managed to prevent the spread of a fire that could have been a great deal worse. All the elevators except one had been locked off on the tenth floor, and that was where they'd been rigged to explode. The charges had been powerful enough to snap the cables and send the cars crashing to the bottom of the shafts, and the saboteur had covered his retreat by flinging a bottle filled with gasoline and a lit fuse against a wall as he fled.

The remaining express elevator had escaped destruction, either because it had been on the ground floor while the saboteur worked or because the man had simply run out of time. Following their instructions, the security guards had not alerted the police, and no one outside the building had reported the explosions; with the size of the structure, it was unlikely that anyone had even heard. Their elusive enemy, Ian thought, seemed to be careful not to call too much attention to his work; apparently, he wanted the fight to be between the families and no one else.

Ian had ordered the express elevator thoroughly checked, but there'd been no sign of tampering. The other elevators stood open on this floor, their bare, smoke-blackened shafts all that was visible, and since the doors had been jammed by the explosions, he had roped them off. He glanced aside where his father stood talking to one of the guards, and braced himself mentally for the struggle he expected to take place.

A few minutes later, as Brandon Stuart joined his son, he said bitterly, "Damn them."

"The Logans aren't responsible," Ian said quietly.

"Oh, for God's sake, Ian—"

Ian turned away from his father and walked down the hall to a lounge area that was partly furnished since this floor had been completed. Some of the security guards and a couple of the company electricians were still grouped around the elevators, and he had no intention of discussing the situation with too many listening ears; at this point, he wasn't sure whom he could trust. He sat down on the arm of a chair and loosened his tie, waiting for his father to join him.

As he did, Brandon said, "Surely you've given up on those fantasies of yours."

"They aren't fantasies, Dad. Someone else is stirring up trouble between the families. Someone who knows just how to use the feud to his own advantage."

"What advantage? Who would have anything to gain by such a scheme?"

"I don't know yet."

Flatly, Brandon said, "I've given you all the time I could, Ian, and you haven't been able to answer that question. So I will. None of our competitors would go this far. Except the Logans. And *they* have everything to gain."

"It isn't them."

"What makes you so damned sure?"

"Because Jon and Michele Logan are working just as hard as I am to prove someone else is involved."

"I don't believe it. No matter what you've heard—"

"Will you listen to me? It is not them. We've agreed both families have an enemy, and it's beginning to look like it isn't a business competitor at all."

"Agreed?" Brandon's eyes narrowed. "You've talked to them about this?"

Very quietly, Ian said, "I'm in love with Michele."

"What?" It was little more than a whisper, genuinely shocked.

Ian kept his own voice quiet and calm. "We met on Martinique. We're going to be married, Dad."

"You're out of your mind."

"No. We're going to be married."

"Do you know what you're saying? Marry a Logan? For God's sake, Ian, sleep with her if you have to, but I'd sooner have a painted whore in the family than that—"

Ian stood up.

For a long moment, Brandon Stuart gazed into the ice-blue eyes of his son, and what he saw there shook him badly. Softly, formally, he said, "I apologize for that remark."

Shaken himself by what he was feeling, by the white-hot rage that had swept through him, Ian turned away and walked over to the windows. He stood with his back to his father, trying to control his anger enough to speak.

"Ian . . . I'm sorry."

"Are you?" He heard the thick sound of his own voice, and cleared his throat harshly. "Sorry for what you said? Or sorry for hating a woman you don't even know?"

Brandon was silent.

Ian laughed shortly and turned to stare at his father. "I want you to understand something. Michele and I are going to be married. For her sake, I hope we can stop this insane feud and live here in peace. For all our sakes, I hope you can accept that. But right now, I don't give a sweet damn whether you do or not. She's the most important thing in my life. Everything else can go straight to hell."

"Including me?" Brandon's voice was mild, his eyes still watchful.

"If that's the way it has to be. I won't fight about

this, Dad. And I won't hear another word against Michele. Ever. Accept it or not, it's up to you."

There was a long silence, tension quivering almost visibly in the air between the two men, and then Brandon said irritably, "Stop glaring at me, Ian." He hesitated, then added a bit dryly, "She must be some lady."

"She is." Ian forced himself to relax, knowing that the critical moment had passed safely, that his father was, at least, resigned. It was what he had hoped for when he'd made it plain he was prepared to sever all ties with his father; a genuine affection aside, Brandon Stuart's sense of family was too strong to allow him to risk losing his only son—no matter what.

"Does Charles Logan know about you two?"

"Not yet."

"It is," Brandon said, "an understatement to say he won't like it."

"That's one reason we're trying to find out who's behind the sabotage. As things stand now, he's convinced it's you and me; one whisper of my relationship with Michele, and she thinks he'll go right over the edge."

"She's right. In fact, I would have expected the same reaction from Jon. I assume he knows?"

"Yes. I think he's suspected for a while; he wasn't very surprised to have it confirmed. He's hardly . . . comfortable with the idea, but he accepts it. He loves his sister too much to lose her over this. And he agrees someone else is involved in the feud."

Brandon went to a chair and sat down, frowning. After a moment, he said, "Which brings me back to the original question. Who?"

Slowly, Ian said, "It's directed at both families,

and the intent is apparently to set us at each other's throats. If it isn't a business competitor—and it's beginning to look like that idea was off base—then it has to be someone who hates both sides." He shook his head. "I don't believe either Jon or myself has made an enemy that rabid, and I know damn well Michele hasn't. Which leaves you and Charles Logan. The two of you must have an enemy in common."

"Besides each other, you mean?" Brandon said wryly.

"Think about it," Ian urged, sure he was on the right track. "There must be someone who has reason to hate you both, and very bitterly. Someone who would go to a great deal of time, trouble, and money in an all-out attempt to destroy you both, by using the feud to his advantage."

Shrugging, Brandon said, "I can't think of anyone I've crossed that badly. I may have been ruthless from time to time in business, but not enough to rouse the kind of hate you're talking about. Maybe he's after Logan alone, and using me as his weapon."

"Maybe. But I think he's after both families. And he's not just ruthless—he's deadly. Jon could have been killed in that explosion; God knows what'll happen next."

"More of the same, I'd guess. Whoever he is, he seems to favor explosives in elevators."

Ian sighed, the various kinds of frustration increasing until he thought he'd explode. "Michele traced the device used on their building to the West Coast, and got a list of buyers; the names don't mean anything to any of us, but one of them may have paid the seller to keep quiet. We're waiting for a description of that man now."

Brandon looked a little surprised, but then said, "I'd forgotten. She is an investigator, isn't she."

Ian nodded, frowning.

"You look worried," his father noted.

"I am. I've just realized a few things. Whoever he is, this bastard knows us. All of us. He has to assume that, given enough time, if Michele suspected a third party she'd have a good chance of finding out who it was; it's what she's trained to do. Now, he's going to realize sooner or later that his plan isn't working, and I'm betting on sooner. He's pushed both sides more than once, and we haven't struck out at each other."

"That isn't like us," Brandon murmured.

"No, it isn't. He could be getting nervous about that, especially if he suspects we're on to him. And the next time he hits . . . he may not aim at a building."

*"Neither way is without tragedy."*

Michele couldn't get that promise out of her head. She and Jon had spoken little during the drive home, both of them aware that what was important had already been said. Their father had been surprised to see them back so early, but neither of them had chosen to tell him about the explosion in the Stuarts' building; he'd find out soon enough.

Michele went upstairs and, instead of getting ready for bed, changed into jeans and a thick sweater. She took her hair down and washed away the makeup. She felt edgy and couldn't seem to get warm. Always, in the forefront of her mind, had been the awareness that someone could be hurt if the feud erupted, but it had occurred to her only tonight that if their common enemy lost patience with the stalemate between the families, he could abandon all caution. And, as Ian had said, he seemed too fond of explosives.

And elevators.

She paced her room restlessly, going over everything in her mind until she could hardly think straight. No matter how hard she tried to come up with answers, only the terrifying possibilities assumed a concrete form. He could decide to turn his attention to people instead of buildings, and if that happened, none of them would be safe.

It was almost midnight when Jon knocked softly on her door and poked his head in. "You have a call," he told her.

"Ian?"

"No. Said his name was Steve. Your contact on the West Coast?"

Quickly, Michele joined her brother out in the hall. "Yes. Where's Dad?"

"He's turned in for the night." Jon followed her down the stairs to the phone in the entrance hall, and stood waiting to hear if there was any new information.

She picked up the phone. "Steve?"

"Sorry to bother you so late, Michele." He sounded more than a little bothered himself.

"Never mind, I was up. Do you have the description?"

"No, that isn't it. Michele . . . I got a very weird message a little while ago. It's supposed to be from the man I've been trying to find again, the one who sold those timers, but I swear it doesn't sound like him."

"What's the message?"

"Got a pencil? You'd better write this down."

Michele found a pencil and pad in the drawer of the small table. "Okay. Ready."

"Here it is: I must warn them. Tell her this immediately. It is vital that she know. Sunday is dangerous. Story I told you was false. Unable to tell you the truth. The buyer is no stranger. Three devices, not one. Only they can stop him. Next days critical."

Frowning down at her neat printing on the pad, Michele said, "That's it?"

"That's it. Block-printed on unlined paper, and signed with scrawled initials. Michele, I never told the man why I was tracing the device, and I never mentioned a woman. But this message . . . it seems to be meant for you."

After a moment, Michele handed the pad to Jon and said, "How was it delivered?"

"Pushed under my door here at home. Which is another weird thing. I heard the bell, and when I went to answer it there was no one there. Just a folded sheet of paper. Since the message was damned specific about Sunday being dangerous, I thought I'd better call you right away."

"I'm glad you did." One statement on the message echoed in her head. Three devices, not one. And two had been used. "I really appreciate it, Steve."

"No problem. Hey—I'll mail the original to you first thing tomorrow. In fact, I'll express it."

"Thanks."

"And if you figure it out," Steve added wryly, "how about letting me in on it? I'm puzzled as hell."

Michele conjured a laugh. "I'll do that."

"Be careful."

"I will." She cradled the receiver slowly and looked

at Jon, who was frowning over the message she'd copied. "Does that make any sense to you?" she asked him.

"Who's it from?"

"Supposedly, the man who sold the timer. But Steve says it doesn't sound like him."

"It sounds damned peculiar," Jon muttered. "She? Did he know you were behind the questions?"

"Not according to Steve." Michele picked up the phone again and called Ian's apartment, so worried that she felt almost sick with it. Three devices . . . band and there was no telling when—or if—that third one would be used. If the saboteur's patience was exhausted, he could have decided to strike twice in one night. The phone rang nearly a dozen times before she broke the connection and tried his office number. No answer. She hung up. "He must still be at the building."

Jon was making a second copy of the message. When he was done, he handed her the original, then glanced at his watch. "Midnight; we're already into Saturday."

"Sunday is dangerous," she murmured, staring down at the message as she read. "Next days critical. How would the man who sold the timer know what his customer meant to do—and when? And why warn us?"

"I don't know. But we can't afford to ignore any warning, no matter who it's from, or why."

"I have to see Ian," Michele said. She was thinking of the message, but that wasn't all that filled her mind. The brief moments they'd shared on the terrace had only sharpened her longing to be with him, and she was haunted by the knowledge that if something were to happen to either of them, he'd never know about their child.

Jon looked at her for a moment, then picked up the phone and called for a cab. "I don't want you driving," he said gruffly when he hung up. "If this bastard can wire elevators, he can wire cars; stay out of yours until I can have it checked over. And use the stairs at Ian's building." He hesitated, then added, "Don't worry if you aren't back by morning. I'll think of something to tell Dad."

She stood on tiptoe to kiss his cheek, but said fiercely, "I hate all this lying!"

"Better than the alternative," Jon pointed out. "At least for now. Besides, Dad may not have a chance to ask about you. It's way past time he was made to listen to a few hard truths. I'll tell him about the sabotage of the Stuarts' building and ask him who could have done it, since we didn't. And I'll hit him with everything else we know. Maybe I can finally get through to him, at least a little."

"We're running out of time."

"I know."

A few minutes later, in a cab heading downtown, Michele wondered for the first time if they were being watched. She wanted to reassure herself that the question was a paranoid one, but after all that had happened she knew it wasn't.

*All around you are the shifting patterns of things seen—and unseen.*

Odd how the fortune teller's predictions kept coming back to her so vividly. As if they had been somehow imprinted on her mind, stamped in her memory but prompted to surface only by some spur she had no conscious control over. She had tried more than once to remember all that had been said, but when she concentrated nothing would come to her except disjointed words and meaningless phrases; it was only when she least expected it that the whispers echoed softly in her mind.

She had no faith in either precognition or predestination; no belief in fortune tellers or fate. But she couldn't escape the uneasy feeling that there was a design to all this, that events were being carefully arranged for a specific purpose. And oddest of all was her impression that more than one hand was involved in the pattern.

She felt like a piece on a chessboard, involved in some obscure struggle for power and moved by the whim and the tactics of an invisible hand.

Roused from the unsettling thoughts by the arrival of her cab at Ian's apartment building, she paid the driver and got out, drawing her coat tighter around her against the cutting force of the rising wind. She hurried into the building, going straight to the security guard's desk.

"Is Mr. Stuart in?" she asked the same man who had been here on that night weeks before.

"No, ma'am. But he said you were to go up any time."

Michele glanced toward the bank of elevators, then located the door to the stairwell nearby. After a slight hesitation, she drew a pen and a small, spiral-ringed notebook from her purse, and jotted a quick note.

"I'll go up," she told the guard, then folded her note and handed it to him. "Will you give him this as soon as he comes in, please?"

"Yes, ma'am." The guard was blessedly incurious, merely accepting the note and saying nothing at all when she headed for the stairwell instead of the elevators. Still, she couldn't help hoping that the man was better at his job than he seemed, or that Ian was responsible for the total lack of curiosity or suspicion where she was concerned.

Ian's apartment was on the eighth floor, but Michele hardly noticed the climb. She let herself into his apartment, realizing only when she was inside that doors could also be wired to explode. It was a sickening realization.

She shrugged out of her coat and left it lying across the couch with her purse, moving restlessly around the neat, quiet living room. She had barely noticed how Ian's home looked the first time she was here, her attention wholly caught up with him and the feelings between them. Now she looked, trying to concentrate, trying not to worry because he wasn't here.

And gradually, as she wandered, she found a kind of peace in what she found. Ties. Connections between them. She found many of her favorite books on his shelves, her favorite music among his records and tapes, prints and watercolors and oils by her favorite artists on his walls. The furnishings were in styles and colors she would have favored, their arrangements lending the spaciousness she preferred.

She settled on the comfortable couch at last, kicking off her shoes and curling up with her cheek resting on a pillow, the sense of him so strongly with her that she felt curiously content and just too tired to think anymore. The edges of fear retreated, and as quiet filled her mind she drifted off to sleep.

At first, she wasn't sure it was a dream, because why on earth would she dream of the striking old man who had stood outside the fortune teller's tent on Martinique? But it had to be a dream, because she knew she was asleep, and he certainly couldn't be here in the apartment even though she saw him clearly when he emerged from a shadowy corner of the room and stood looking down at her with gentle eyes.

*"Have courage, child. It's nearly over now."*

She wanted to ask him who he was and why he was here, but some part of her understood those answers without having to hear them. He was the hand of destiny, she realized, and his was both a kinder and a more compassionate touch than she had believed, guidance rather than compulsion. He was light and dark, yin and yang, creative and receptive, forever at odds, forever united, a divided force connected only by a fragile thread, seeking wholeness, struggling for harmony, fighting for love.

Are you? she asked, or thought she asked.

*"How poetic you make it sound!"* He was amused but kindly and with understanding. *"I am Fortune, child. A roll of the dice, a turn of the card, a fork in the road."*

Are you doing this to us?

*"I only watch. And try to help. You have all the pieces now. The answers are within reach."* He glanced aside, as if some sound had drawn his attention, then looked back at her with his gentle, unutterably sweet smile. *"Courage,"* he repeated.

Michele opened her eyes with a start, feeling her heart thudding as she sat up. A glance at the clock glowing on Ian's stereo told her that less than an hour had passed. She looked around warily. Empty. The room was empty. It had only been a dream, of course, prompted by her own unsettled thoughts of fate and destiny. She drew a shaky breath of relief, but even then couldn't shake the sense of presence, couldn't totally dismiss the notion that he *had* been there, that strange old man, coming to her out of the night because he'd somehow known she was at the end of her rope and needed reassurance.

Of all the wild, impossible ideas . . .

"Michele?"

She hadn't heard him come in, but at the sound of his voice she jumped up from the couch and hurried to meet him. His arms closed about her instantly, lifting her off her feet as he held her tightly against him.

"I was so worried about you," she whispered. "He bought three devices, Ian. There's one he hasn't used yet."

"Three? Are you sure?"

"Steve got a message tonight from the man who sold them, and he called me at home—"

"Easy," Ian soothed, setting her back on her feet and kissing her gently. She was trembling, clearly strained to the breaking point, and he couldn't bear to see her that way. Even a diamond could be shattered if the blow fell in just the right place, and Michele had already withstood too much.

He guided her to the couch and sat down, drawing her into his lap and holding her. "You're tired. Just rest for a little while," he murmured into the soft, dark cloud of her hair. "We'll get through this, baby, I promise."

Clinging to him, she said unsteadily, "It just hit me tonight, all at once, that anything could happen now. Then the message came, and it didn't make sense, but I had to tell you about it. Jon called a cab for me because he wants to check my car out, and he told me not to take the elevator here—"

Michele broke off and drew a deep breath, trying to quiet her own surging emotions. But they wouldn't quiet. For the first time, she felt her own exhaustion, the strain of too much worry and fear held taut for too long, but it wasn't rest or sleep she needed, and she felt that, too. She needed to be with the man she loved, just be with him; she needed to draw strength from the certainty of their feelings.

Raising her head from his shoulder, Michele looked into his beautiful warm eyes, and her heart was thudding so hard she thought it would burst. "I don't need to rest," she whispered. "I need you."

Ian touched her cheek tenderly, and then his hand slid around to the nape of her neck, beneath the soft weight of her hair. He kissed her, the first gentleness disappearing rapidly as she made no effort to hide her own taut desire. Her mouth opened under his, her hands going to his neck as she moved restlessly in his lap, and a soft sound tangled in the back of her throat.

His concern for her had prompted gentleness rather than desire, but as always her honest need for him instantly ignited his own passion. It had been too long; no matter how urgent the worries and dangers surrounding them, once they were together nothing else seemed to matter.

He carried her to his bedroom, and to his bed. They were both too wound up to allow patience, too eager for one another to permit a slow joining. Clothing was flung aside carelessly in the lamplit quiet of the room, and they fell on the bed together.

"Love me," she whispered, trembling under the onslaught of his hungry caresses, burning with the feverish, all-consuming need to belong to him. The time apart had caged that necessity, but now it burst free like something alive and on the wing, and she gloried in the freedom of it.

He was murmuring to her, husky words of love and desire, his hands shaking as he touched her, and when he eased into her they both caught their breath raggedly.

Michele totally lost control in his arms, and she didn't care. The pleasure was so intense it was like being drawn into a whirlpool of sensation, a quickening spiral that wound tighter and tighter until she couldn't breathe, couldn't stop the sounds escaping her, couldn't do anything except cling to him wildly and cry out as all her senses shattered.

# Nine

"Can you stay?" Ian asked quietly.

"Yes." She would have stayed even if it had been impossible, because she needed to be with him too badly to leave him. "Jon's going to have it out with Dad first thing in the morning, so he probably won't even notice I'm not there. If he does notice, Jon said he'd cover for me."

"I'm beginning to like your brother very much."

"He's been a bit of a surprise," Michele admitted. "I think he saw how badly I wanted to be with you right now, and he seems worried about how I'm holding up."

"You're too thin," Ian murmured, his fingers gently probing the tiny indentations between her ribs.

They were lying close together, and he was propped on an elbow as he gazed down at her. Michele opened her eyes slowly and looked up at him, relaxed now and feeling both stronger and more content than she had in weeks. She took his hand and guided it to rest on her lower stomach.

"I won't be for long," she said softly.

He actually paled, his darkening eyes fixed on their hands both resting over her slender body. His fingers moved slightly, almost compulsively, as if he were seeking signs that wouldn't be visible for weeks yet.

"You're sure?" he asked huskily.

"Yes. Do you mind?" She was watching his face intently, certain of his response but needing reassurance as any woman does at such a time. And she found it when his gaze lifted to hers, his eyes still dark and filled with tenderness and a moving look of wonder.

"Michele . . ." He kissed her, a slow, warm, drugging kiss that was love and delight and a purely male pride.

Understanding that last emotion made Michele laugh softly as her arms went up around his neck. "Didn't you think you had it in you?" she asked.

He chuckled as well, gathering her even closer against him. "I didn't know. You said there was a good chance, but that was weeks ago."

"As near as I could figure it," Michele said dryly, "that twenty-four hours we were together on Martinique was the perfect time for me to get pregnant. In fact, it was the only time all month I *could* have. My doctor once told me that he never recommended the rhythm method of birth control because it was so undependable, but that it would probably be as effective for me as the pill." Suddenly grave, she added, "It wasn't deliberate though, Ian. I hope you know that."

Just as seriously, he said, "There were two of us there, remember? I'm just as responsible for not taking precautions. In fact, when you told me it could have already happened, I wondered if maybe that's what I wanted. Now I'm sure. I love you, Michele Logan. And I want our child very, very much."

It was some time later before Michele could rouse herself from the blissful warmth that had surrounded them both, but she made the effort even though it cost her a pang to bring up what had to be faced. It wasn't over yet, and until it was the stolen moments with Ian couldn't be all peaceful ones.

"That message," she murmured. "You have to see it. There's a warning about Sunday. And next week. The copy I made is in my purse."

"I'll go get it," Ian said, clearly reluctant to leave her as he slid from the bed.

She banked pillows and sat up against them, absently drawing the covers higher. It was doubtful either of them would sleep before dawn, she knew, if then. And even though the last weeks had left her tired, just being with Ian gave her the energy and stamina she needed.

Besides that, their time together was too precious to waste in sleep, she decided.

While she waited for Ian to return, she thought about the strange dream she'd had, frowning a little over the peculiar things that had been said. Was her subconscious trying to tell her that all the pieces were there, right in front of her to see? She supposed that was the only explanation, but it still puzzled her that her subconscious had taken the form of an odd old man she had seen only once, weeks ago, outside a fortune teller's tent on Martinique.

Fortune teller . . . *I am Fortune.*

Well, maybe it made sense after all. Of a sort. She closed her eyes and tried to remember the predictions once again, but all she got were disjointed phrases. Two paths . . . neither way without tragedy . . . seeds sown . . . bitter fruit . . . cannot change what must be . . . the truth you feel. . . .

Opening her eyes and frowning across Ian's bedroom, she told herself yet again that it was absurd to look for answers in the meaningless words of a self-proclaimed psychic. She'd have better odds rolling dice.

*A roll of the dice, a turn of the card, a fork in the road.*

Twenty-six relatively blameless years, Michele thought with a surge of rebellion, and now she was surrounded by a great deal too much cryptic nonsense. Fortune tellers and faceless enemies and mysterious messages.

"Why are you frowning?" Ian asked as he came in.

"Because nothing makes sense." She looked at him, and couldn't help but grin. "Although I must admit, being served a snack in bed by a naked man at three A.M. is certainly nothing to frown at. I could get used to this."

Chuckling, he placed the heavily laden tray on the bed and crawled in beside her. The tray held an assortment of cheese, crackers, fresh fruit, and various other snacks, as well as two tall glasses of milk. Ian handed her one of the glasses and clinked his against it very gravely.

"I was starving, and I noticed you didn't eat much at the party. Besides that, you can't tell me your doctor didn't scold you for losing weight."

"He just mentioned it in passing," Michele murmured.

"I'll bet."

Michele took refuge in her milk and wrinkled her nose after the first sip. "I never did like this stuff."

"Drink it," Ian said, and fed her a cracker before she could protest.

She laughed at him but felt warmed by his concern. Conscious of an appetite for the first time in days, she ate enough to satisfy him, and then they both continued to snack while he frowned over her copy of the odd message.

"As paranoid as it sounds," she offered after a few minutes, "do you think this could possibly be a ruse of some kind, a trick from the very man we're after? Or am I hearing the wrong kind of hoofbeats?"

Ian blinked, then nodded as he understood the reference. "When you hear hoofbeats, think horses, not zebras?"

"Right."

"The most likely explanation is usually the correct one," he noted thoughtfully. "It's a little hard to believe that whoever's against us would go to all the trouble of warning us, and putting us on guard. At the same time, I'm having a problem believing that the shady character who sold the timers would send a message like this one—apparently aimed directly at you."

"That's one of the things I can't figure out," she muttered, nibbling on an apple that Ian had cored and sliced. "Steve swears he never mentioned a woman, never even said he was trying to get information for someone else."

Ian studied the message. "The buyer is no stranger," he read slowly. "No stranger to the seller? Or to us? Sunday is dangerous, next days critical. Only they can stop him."

"Weird, isn't it?" Something else about the message was bothering her, something she couldn't make come clear in her mind. The sentences themselves were wrong, she thought, misleading in a way she couldn't put her finger on, as if there was a pattern that she was missing.

"What does Jon think?"

"That we can't afford to ignore any warning, no matter how enigmatic it is, or whom it comes from."

"He's right. We'll all have to be especially careful tomorrow, and somehow figure out why next week is critical."

Michele looked at him worriedly. "How can we be more careful than we have been? How do we guard against a lunatic with a habit of hiring middlemen to plant explosives? Whether we believe the message or not, we have to assume there's another timer—or some kind of device—that hasn't been used yet. Being on guard and having good security hasn't stopped him so far; he could booby-trap anything."

"About all we *can* do is take cabs and stay out of elevators." Ian shook his head. "Why elevators? First the one in your family's building, and then ours last night. If he just wanted to stall completion of the buildings—or make it look that way—then why choose elevators as his targets?"

Michele had been around the construction business long enough to see what he was getting at. "It is strange," she agreed slowly. "There are a hundred other things he could have done. Sabotage the electrical systems, the air conditioning, the plumbing— any of those would have taken a lot more time and money to repair, and the damage would have been more widespread."

"We're missing something," Ian said. "I don't

know what it is, but there's a key somewhere. I asked Dad last night if he and your father had an enemy in common—"

A sudden chill shot through Michele, and she stiffened. "That's it," she breathed unsteadily as the words surfaced vividly in her mind. " 'Even now, the seeds sown decades ago grow twisted to bear a dark and bitter fruit.' *Decades* ago."

"One of the fortune teller's predictions?" Ian asked, guessing from the phrasing.

"Yes. And now it makes sense. Ian, you know the history of our families as well as I do."

"Probably. The point being?"

"For every generation, the hatred was an inherited thing, a family matter rather than a personal grudge. But somehow, it always *became* personal. And so the feud was maintained, each generation hating for their own reasons. Right?"

"As far as I can remember, that sounds right. Until we came along, that is."

Still marveling at the quirk of fate that had prompted her meeting with Ian on an island so far away, she leaned over to kiss him. "I'm so glad we came along."

"So am I," he murmured, touching her cheek gently.

Michele forced herself to think of less pleasant things. "But before we did—thirty-five years ago, to be exact—something happened between our fathers. I'm willing to bet that until then, they didn't feel much personal animosity, but after that they hated each other."

"Do you know what happened?"

"I got part of the story from Jon, but I don't think he knows all of it. You were right, it was a woman. Apparently, both our fathers fell in love with her. From that point, I'm not sure of the facts. She was with Dad for a while, then told him she loved your father more and went to him. But something happened; Jon said there was a confrontation of some kind, and she ended up without either of them."

Ian leaned back against the pillows and frowned. "You think this woman could be behind the sabotage?"

Michele drew a breath. "I think we'd better find out what happened to her. Maybe our fathers gave her a reason to hate. Maybe the *why* of all this . . . is revenge."

After a long moment, Ian said, "I'll get the story out of Dad. I have a feeling he'll be more willing to talk about it than your father. Besides that, Dad knows about us."

"He does?" A bit warily, she added, "How did he take it?"

"On the whole, fairly well." He smiled at her. "Not delighted—but resigned."

Ruefully, Michele said, "Then we've done better than I ever expected. Your father and my brother have survived the shock. If Jon gets through to Dad in the morning . . ."

Ian glanced at the clock on his nightstand. "It's already morning." He leaned forward to get the tray and set it on the floor by the bed. "You need to rest."

Michele cuddled up to his side, but as he reached out to turn off the lamp, she said thoughtfully, "I'm not all that tired."

Enough light filtered through the drapes for Ian to see the catlike gleam of her haunting eyes. "No?"

"Well, no. Maybe it was the milk."

He realized that his hands were stroking her delicate body, the soft flesh of her throat drawing his lips as if to a lodestar. Half groaning, he said against her warm skin, "I've said it from the first; you make me so crazy I can't even remember my own good intentions."

"What good intentions?" she murmured, but not as if the subject interested her.

"Letting you rest, baby." He lifted his head, looking down at her with burning eyes.

Michele wound her arms around his neck and kissed him. "I'll sleep late," she promised softly.

It was late when she woke up, Michele knew that even before she opened her eyes. She also knew that she woke reluctantly, and it took her several moments to realize that a ringing telephone was the culprit. She lay with her head on Ian's shoulder and listened drowsily as he talked, not really trying to figure out what was said until he moved slightly to replace the receiver in its cradle on the nightstand.

"Oedipus," she murmured. Her pillow shifted as Ian chuckled.

"What?"

"Or Electra. It's a complex. Psychology." She lifted her head and stared at him owlishly. "No. That's between parents and children. What is it between siblings?"

"I have no idea," Ian said politely. "No idea what you're talking about, and no idea what 'it' is between siblings since I don't have any."

Michele's drifting thoughts finally settled, and she made the connection. "Ah. My brother calling my lover while I'm in my lover's bed. It must have started a train of thought." She considered that, then added bemusedly, "I think the train derailed."

Ian was laughing. He raised his head from the pillow and kissed her. "You're very interesting to wake up with, you know that? I remember on Martinique you woke up once saying, 'When I haven't any blue, I use red.' When I asked you what you were talking about, you said Picasso."

She frowned. "I wonder what brought that on. There's usually a germ of an idea in there somewhere."

"As in Oedipus?"

"I guess. That was Jon on the phone, wasn't it?"

"Yes. And if he was feeling any brotherly jealousies, he didn't let on. I told him about your idea that this whole thing may have started thirty-five years ago, and that I was going to call my father and get the facts. He said once you had a name, you could probably trace the woman. Apparently his morning confrontation was less than successful, since your father hardly listened before storming out of the house in a rage. He also said your absence hadn't been noticed, and that we all needed to talk about the situation. I certainly agreed. He'll be here in about an hour."

Michele peered past Ian at the clock on the nightstand. "Eleven. Even after all that food in the wee hours, I'm starving. Can we eat while we talk?"

They could, although Ian was still preparing the meal when Michele went to let Jon in. She was staving off hunger with a slice of hot French bread, and at her brother's surprised look said lightly, "It's all Ian's fault; he primed the pump."

"Should I ask what you're talking about?" Jon wanted to know, looking around the apartment with wary interest.

"My appetite. Ian fed me at three o'clock this

morning, and it seems to have triggered my appe-tite. For the first time in weeks, I'm hungry. Come on into the kitchen; lunch is almost ready. Have you eaten?" She kept her voice casual deliberately, aware that her brother was a little uncomfortable and trying to make it easier on him.

"Not since breakfast." Jon followed her into the spacious and well-equipped kitchen, and his faint amusement grew as he saw Ian skillfully at work preparing spaghetti. Nearby on the counter was an assortment of greens for salad, which Michele re-turned to as she finished her slice of bread.

Ian glanced at him, saying merely, "Coffee's over there by Michele; wine's on the table. Help yourself."

Jon chose wine, then sat at the table and watched the activity in silence. Even though he said nothing, the room wasn't silent, because Michele and Ian were clearly in the middle of an amiable discussion concerning his skills—and her lack thereof—in the kitchen. As he watched and listened, Jon felt a pang of envy. The relationship between the two was so close it was a tangible thing, as if they dovetailed perfectly.

He knew they were as worried about the dan-gers surrounding them as he was, yet they seemed curiously insulated, as if the love they shared was a kind of shield. His last misgivings about the rela-tionship faded, and he could only feel something like awe at the knowledge that with all the genera-tions of five hundred years ranged against them, they had found each other.

A few minutes later, Michele unconsciously echoed her brother's thoughts by proposing a wry toast before they began eating. "To destiny," she said, raising her glass.

The two men gravely touched their glasses to hers, and it was Ian who said, "Are you still thinking of the fortune teller?"

"Well, dammit, she's gotten more right than wrong." While they ate, Michele told Jon about the visit on Martinique, and how one of the predictions made had prompted her to think of what had happened thirty-five years ago.

"Right now," Jon said when she'd finished, "I can't think of a better idea. It's a long time to wait for revenge, though."

"Maybe it took time to plan. And to raise the money. This has cost somebody plenty."

Ian nodded in agreement. "Once we eliminate business competition, it pretty much has to be a personal grudge. And our fathers have hated each other as long as any of us can remember; if the beginning of that hatred hurt someone else, then that's a good place to look for a common enemy."

Jon looked at him. "Have you talked to your father about it yet?"

"No." Ian glanced at his watch, and then pushed back his chair and rose. "I'll call him now." He went out into the living room to use that extension.

He was a little surprised when his father resisted talking about the subject; no matter how he argued, he couldn't get anything out of the older man except the bare facts of the woman's name and when she had left Atlanta.

"We may be on to something," he told Jon and Michele as he rejoined them in the kitchen. "Dad sure as hell didn't want to talk about it; it was like pulling teeth just to get a name out of him."

"But you got that much?" Michele asked.

"Barely. Her name was Helen Gordon, and she

left Atlanta exactly thirty-five years ago this past June."

"Any idea where she went?" Jon wondered.

"Not really. Although Dad did say he thought she was originally from somewhere on the West Coast. An interesting coincidence, isn't it?"

They looked at one another for a moment, and then Ian asked Michele, "Think you can track her?"

"There isn't much to go on but, given time, I think I can. Driver's license, social security number—most people have both those. If she didn't change her name or try to cover her tracks in some other way. But I'll need to use the computer in my office."

"Your office building's closed on Saturday," Jon noted.

"Security will let me in. It wouldn't be the first time I've worked during the weekend."

Ian and Jon exchanged glances, and the former said, "Then we'll all go."

Michele didn't object. With the threat against them all, she knew she'd worry constantly with Ian or her brother out of her sight. She was more than ever conscious of time ticking away, and was convinced that if they could only find out who was behind the attack on both families they would be able to find a way to stop the destruction.

"Where's Dad?" she asked Jon as they all rode to her office building in a cab.

"Where he usually is on Saturday. The golf course."

That relieved her mind somewhat. They were, she knew, tempting fate by being together downtown where they were known by sight to too many people. Even on a Saturday.

Tempting fate. The entire situation seemed to

revolve around a fateful sequence of events, Michele thought. If they were right about what had happened decades ago, the beginnings were there; the old feud burned more brightly than ever after some conflict ended in hatred. Then a son and daughter of the right ages born to different sides, neither of whom was steeped in the bitterness of their families quite as much as they could have been. A lifetime of knowing each other from a distance, and an unexpected meeting on an island paradise far away from their homes.

What were the odds against that, Michele wondered, that she and Ian would meet unexpectedly in a place where their attraction could be nurtured? And, even more, the odds against love growing where so much mistrust and suspicion had been sown?

Was it fate, after all? Had the hand of destiny always meant her to love Ian, to forge a bridge between families at war for five centuries?

Michele was a sensible woman, her beliefs for the most part grounded firmly in reality. But it disturbed her to realize how many random factors had woven themselves into a pattern so complex and bewildering. If a single thread had snapped, the pattern couldn't have held. If she had not met Ian, not loved him enough to trust him; if Jon had not been able to at least see the possibility of a common enemy; if that enemy had not chosen to use a state of the art device still new enough to be traced with relative ease; if a fortune teller had not made predictions so uncannily appropriate that they seemed to Michele a set of clues to the puzzle . . .

If. If all those connections had not been made, the feud would now rage more bitterly than ever, probably with violence and destruction on both sides.

Michele didn't realize how long she had been silent until Ian helped her from the cab in front of her office building and asked quietly, "Are you all right?"

She looked up at him and Jon as they stood on the pavement, and managed a smile. "I was just thinking of . . . connections."

Ian squeezed her hand as if he understood, then said, "There's one connection we don't want made just yet; we'd better get off the street."

Michele agreed with that. With the fateful twists that had already taken place, it would be all too ironically perfect for some roving journalist to see a startling sight on a downtown street corner and make the right connection.

The security guard let them into the building, as unsurprised by Michele's appearance as she'd expected. He knew Jon by sight and accepted both Ian and Michele's offhand explanation of needed research without a blink.

By tacit consent, they took the stairs rather than the elevator, a minor inconvenience since Michele's office was on the fourth floor. The hall was deserted when they emerged from the stairwell, office doors closed and a high-countered reception desk near the elevators unoccupied.

Michele led the way to her office and got out her keys to unlock the door. But, with the key inserted, she suddenly went still.

"What?" Ian asked immediately.

"It isn't locked. Jon, didn't I lock up yesterday?"

He nodded.

Leaving the key in the door, she stepped back. "Maybe we should err on the side of caution."

"Definitely," Ian said grimly. "None of us is going in there until we're sure it's safe."

Michele took a deep breath and made herself think for a moment, then said, "I think my brain's in neutral. The security cameras. This way." She led them back down the hall to the reception desk.

"You have a camera in your office?" Jon asked as she went around behind the desk. "I've never noticed it."

"You weren't supposed to," Michele said. "This is an insurance company, remember? One of the things we do is recommend security systems to clients who want us to insure them; the better the system, the less chance we have of taking a loss. This building's full of gadgets, because the president thinks we should practice what we preach."

She pressed a button on an enigmatic keypad built into the lower level of the desk, and a panel opened to reveal three small monitor screens. The two men joined her as she activated the camera in her office by pushing another button, and the center screen came alive with a flicker.

The screen showed a neat desk at first, the camera holding steady. Michele pressed more buttons, and the image shifted slowly as the camera panned around the office. For several minutes, she maneuvered the camera remotely so that they were offered a clear view of the door and the walls near it. Finally, she straightened with a sigh.

"Nothing. The door's clear."

Even so, it was Ian and Jon who went into the office first, neither of them giving Michele a chance to argue. The small room appeared peaceful, but both the men began to search methodically. After a few moments, Michele began to think they were all being ridiculously paranoid, and had started toward her desk where Ian was looking when his voice stopped her cold.

"Michele, get out of here."

"What is it?" she whispered.

Ian had eased open the bottom drawer of her desk, where files were normally kept, and was staring down into it. "Another one of those damned timers. There's five minutes left on the clock. Get out of here!"

Her heart was beating so fast it seemed to echo inside her head, but she forced herself to think clearly. Five minutes. Five minutes could be a very long time.

It could also be no time at all.

Steadily, she said, "There isn't enough time to call in someone to disarm it. We'll have to do it."

"Great," Jon muttered, joining Ian to stare down at the deceptively innocent-looking device.

"If it's the same device he used before, I studied all the diagrams and specifications. It can only be detonated when the timer reaches zero; you could throw it out a window and it wouldn't go off until then. I know what to do." Her eyes held Ian's as he looked up, and she went around the desk to join them.

Tautly, Ian said, "When this thing gets to a minute, we're out of here—disarmed or not."

"Agreed," Jon said instantly.

Michele took a long look at the device and sighed in unconscious relief. "It's the same one. But all I see is the timer; where are the explosives?" That, she knew, was the critical question. If their enemy had gotten as fancy with his explosives as he had with the timer, they were in trouble. If, on the other hand, either dynamite or plastique had been used, preventing an explosion would be simple.

Ian carefully pushed aside the files still in the

drawer, and they all saw two thin red wires extending from the timer toward the back and out of sight. He followed the wires by touch, reaching all the way into the drawer without pulling it out any farther. "Out the back of the drawer," he said. "I can't tell where they go beyond that."

"Under the desk," Jon said, and knelt to peer beneath. An instant later, his voice strained, he said, "I can't see the wires, it's too dark. But there's something wedged into two corners. It looks like plastique."

Instantly, Michele said, "Find the wires and pull them out of the plastique; as long as the timer isn't connected to the explosives, nothing can happen." Unless, of course, there was another surprise planned. It would have been stupid to bank on anything where their enemy was concerned.

"Three minutes," Ian said.

Jon reached under the desk and probed. "There's one. Where the hell's the other one? Wait—got it." He emerged with the two red wires in his hand.

The LED indicator of the timer continued to count off the seconds methodically.

Jon rose to his feet, leaving the wires lying a safe distance from the plastique, and dusted off his hands precisely. "I suggest we wait outside," he said with unnatural calm.

"You won't get an argument," Ian said, taking Michele's hand and guiding her from behind the desk.

They picked the farthest spot from Michele's office—the stairwell—and waited there. Ian kept his gaze fixed on his watch, but held Michele close to his side as the seconds ticked away. "Three . . . two . . . one . . . zero," he murmured.

The silence was unbroken. After another eternal five minutes, Ian sighed roughly and hugged Michele hard.

Jon was leaning back against the wall with his hands in his pockets, his face as pale as those of the other two. He looked at his sister and said very politely, "I'll never again give you a hard time about your job."

Michele was trying to quit shaking, her face pressed against Ian's chest, but at that masterly statement couldn't hold back a watery laugh.

Sometime later, after the plastique had been removed from her desk and stored with relative safety in a thick metal box Michele found in the storeroom, she sat in her chair and watched as Ian and Jon examined the timer.

"What I'd like to know," Ian said, "is how the bastard activated the timer. He doesn't seem to have much trouble getting into security-conscious buildings, but how would he know when to set the clock? He couldn't have known we'd be here, or when we would be."

"He's watching," Michele told them. "That timer can be activated remotely. All he had to do was get in here to set the explosives, and then stand by outside until we came into the building. Or until I did."

Ian frowned. "You think he was after you alone?"

She drew a breath. "I think so. Because if he was after all three of us, then he expected us to be together, and that doesn't make sense."

"How do you mean?" Jon asked.

"Look at his apparent plan. Divide and conquer; he's been out to set the Logans and Stuarts at each other's throats from the start. Now, I could accept that he realized we were working together and decided to eliminate all three of us, but I would have thought he'd have asked himself first of all *why* we're working together."

"And if he did," Ian said slowly, "he might have found out about you and me."

"Oh, hell," Jon muttered as he realized.

Michele nodded. "If he knows, and if he wants to push Dad over the edge, he has a perfect weapon. Why bother to blow us up? Tell Dad about Ian and me, and then he can just sit back and watch."

"We're out of time," Ian said.

She turned on her computer and stared at the blank screen as the machine warmed up. "Even if he doesn't know for sure," she murmured, "the sight of us together might give him ideas. And it won't take any more than a hint to Dad."

Michele got to work. With so little information about Helen Gordon, it was a slow process, and since data storage by computer was a fairly recent thing, a large number of older records hadn't yet been converted into sophisticated electronics. Michele made several phone calls, but she had to resort to personal contacts made over the past few years because few record-keeping facilities boasted weekend business hours. And more than once, a computer hacker who owed her a favor—or wanted one owed to him—gave up an access code never meant to be public.

Around four o'clock, Jon went out and brought back food and drinks for them, and Michele ate while she worked. The men talked quietly at first, then later poured over the information that began chattering from her printer. Michele was tapping into every source she could think of, assigning some to the printer and some to her screen, but it wasn't until nearly six o'clock that the information began falling into place.

"I've got a record of a California driver's license. Helen Gordon, a Los Angeles address. It expired almost ten years ago, and was never renewed, but the address is the same going back more than thirty years." Michele looked up, frowning.

"Is she the right Helen Gordon?" Jon asked. They had already located and discounted several of that name.

Ian, who was studying a printout of students registered in the Atlanta area colleges and universities thirty-five years before, suddenly asked, "What's that address?"

Michele glanced at her screen and rattled it off.

"Bingo. You were right; she must have come out here to go to college. Listed as a transfer student from Los Angeles, and at just the right time. Dropped out in the spring quarter thirty-five years ago this past April. No reason given."

Within the next half hour, they found more indications that they were on the right track, and when Michele uncovered a coroner's report dated ten years previously, there was little doubt they had found the right woman.

She read the information on her screen, then sat back in her chair feeling a curious little chill. She looked at the waiting men and said flatly, "Helen Gordon died ten years ago, in an accident. An elevator cable snapped."

"So at least now we know why it's been elevators," Ian said tiredly. "But if she's dead, who's after us? A husband? Offspring?"

Michele stared at him for a long moment as a

final connection was made in her mind, then muttered, "Oh, damn . . ." and began very quickly typing commands into her computer. With the right question finally asked, the answer came through in minutes. Even so, Michele couldn't believe the answer though it made all too much sense.

"Michele?" Ian leaned forward, his eyes concerned. "What is it? You've gone white."

"Oedipus," she said dully. "I must have already known. I just didn't make the right connection this morning."

Jon looked totally bewildered. "What?"

"The love of a boy for his mother, his jealousy of his father. And a hundred times worse for him if she was bitter." Michele drew a deep breath and said, "We know Helen Gordon left here in June of that year. Six months later—exactly thirty-five years ago on this coming Monday—she gave birth to a son. She wasn't married; maybe that was why she combined two family names for his. According to his birth certificate, he was named Nicholas Gordon South."

"Our mysterious buyer," Jon said, then realized that Michele and Ian were thinking along different lines. It was in both their faces. "What?" he demanded.

Softly, Michele said, "Six months later, Jon. That's when her son was born. Six months after leaving here, after being involved with both our father and Ian's. I wonder if Nicholas Gordon even knows which name is rightfully his."

After a long moment, Jon said, "You mean we could have a half brother who's trying to destroy us?"

"We could. Or Ian could. I find it a little unlikely that she could have been involved with a third man at just that time. One of them must have fathered her son."

Jon began to swear steadily in a low voice and without inflection.

"What about Gordon?" Ian asked Michele. "Can you trace him? He's still faceless as far as we're concerned."

Michele set to work, forcing herself to concentrate because the alternative was too painful. But she couldn't help thinking that the fortune teller's warning had been all too terribly accurate. The seeds sown decades ago *had* borne a dark and bitter fruit.

The only cause for Helen Gordon's son to have launched such an all-out campaign to destroy the Logan and Stuart families had to be that he hated them both. Michele was convinced that the blood of at least one side of the feud ran in his veins, and he was prepared to destroy both sides in his bitterness.

# Ten

Within another hour, Michele knew she'd lost the trail. Nicholas Gordon South had simply ceased to exist when his mother died ten years before. The family home she had lived in until her death was sold, and her son vanished. If he changed his name, he didn't do so legally in California; if he held down a job or dealt with any of the myriad institutions requiring valid identification, he did so under another name.

"It's no use," she said finally, leaning back and rubbing her tense neck slowly. "He might as well have dropped off the face of the earth."

"Enough," Ian said, going around the desk to take her hands and pull her gently to her feet. "You're exhausted. You haven't taken a break in hours."

The telephone on Michele's desk shrilled abruptly, interrupting Ian and making her jump. After an instant, she leaned over and picked up the instrument.

"Hello?"

"Michele, it's Jackie. Jon said you might have to work on something today, so I thought—"

"Jackie, what's wrong?" Her friend sounded shaken, as if she'd been crying.

"I—I went by your house a little while ago. Your father was—I've never seen him like that. He was storming around yelling at Leona to pack your things because you weren't coming back to his house. Michele . . . somebody told him about you and Ian, that you were together on Martinique. Leona said there was a call, and he just went crazy—"

The phone slipped from Michele's nerveless fingers, and Jon quickly reached over to grab it and ask Jackie what was wrong.

Ian pulled Michele into his arms and held her gently, his face grim. "Baby . . ."

"I knew it would hurt," she said quietly, looking up at him. "I knew that. But not like this." She felt shattered, wounded, as if someone had reached into her and opened a vein. "How can people . . . hate so much? He's my *father*."

Ian wanted to reassure her that it would be all right. He wanted to wipe away the lost anguish in her haunting eyes, shield her from a blow she should never have had to bear. But he couldn't. All he could do was hold her.

Michele clung to him, not crying because the hurt went too deep for that easy release. This was the risk she had faced, that the cost of her bond with Ian would be the severing of the ties between her and her father. She had known it was possible, even probable, but she had hoped from the beginning that it wouldn't happen. Even now, she couldn't quite believe it had happened, and some part of her refused to accept it.

Jon hung up the phone, his face pale. Speaking directly to Ian, he said, "She'd better stay with you. From the sound of it, Dad's really gone over the edge." With suppressed violence, he added, "Dammit, this time he's going to listen to me if I have to knock him down and sit on him."

Michele turned her head to look at her brother, though she didn't draw away from Ian. "Be careful."

Nodding, Jon said, "I'll call and let you know." Then he hurried out of the office.

There was a moment of silence, and then Michele looked at Ian and said fiercely, "I love you. No matter what happens, that isn't going to change."

"I love you, too, baby." He held her a moment longer, then reached out to get her coat. "Come on. There's nothing else we can do now."

For the first time, Michele realized that it was night, that darkness had fallen while they'd worked. She was very tired, and the pain of her father's reaction had been encased in numbness. It occurred to her that if it had to happen, better this way; if she had looked into her father's eyes and seen what he was feeling as he disowned her, it might well have been a sight from which she would never have recovered.

Ian took her back to his apartment, and took care of her. He warmed soup and insisted she eat it, then put her to bed and joined her even though it was still early. And this time, it wasn't a matter of good intentions. She was exhausted and numb, he was weary, and the comfort they found together was in simply holding each other.

"Will you *listen* to me!" Jon demanded, having to raise his voice just to be heard over his father's roaring.

Charles Logan wasn't making sense and hadn't been for some time. The pressures that had been building inside him over the last weeks, pressures contained by Jon's own persuasion, had finally escaped. Being told by a whispery voice on the telephone that his daughter had acquired a lover on Martinique would have been enough to upset him terribly; the additional information that the lover was none other than Ian Stuart had been a bone-jarring shock so devastating and enraging that he was in serious danger of suffering a stroke.

He was pacing his study, his movements violent and uncontrolled, so wrapped up in his own bitter fury that he was barely aware of Jon's presence. "I won't have it," he muttered, his voice hoarse from all the yelling. "I'll ruin the bastards, both of them. I'll see them lose everything they have. And *her*! How could she do this to me? . . . She knows what they are, she *knows*. I've taught her—"

Jon grabbed his father's arm and quite literally pushed him into a chair near the big desk. "Taught her?" His voice was bitter. "Oh, you did your best. You did all you could to teach both of us to hate. And you almost succeeded. I hated Ian so much it was like a sickness, eating away at me—until my bright, beautiful sister had the guts to make me wonder *why*."

Charles stared up at him, a flash of bewilderment momentarily showing in his eyes. "Why? For God's sake, Jon—"

"God had nothing to do with it," Jon snapped. "And Ian had nothing to do with it. Just you. Just you and five hundred years of hate. Before I was even old enough to understand what hate was, you were filling me with it, making the Stuart name a curse so dirty it burned in my throat."

"They're our enemies!"

"*No.*" Jon grasped the arms of his father's chair and leaned down, no more than a foot separating two furious faces. "We pick our enemies, Dad. And we choose our friends. Only our families are chosen for us. But you couldn't stand that, couldn't bear to think I might not hate where you did. So you didn't wait to find out if your enemy was mine—you made sure of it. And I'll forever regret the fact that I *let* you, even though Ian has never done one single damned thing to make him my enemy."

"He's trying to stall the project, him and his father—"

"Are you so blind with hate that you can't see the truth no matter how big it is? Who sabotaged *their* building, Dad? Who planted a bomb hours ago that just missed killing Michele, me—*and* Ian? Do you have an answer for that?"

For the first time, Charles Logan was silenced, bewilderment growing stronger in his eyes because he didn't have an answer.

Jon straightened slowly and stared down at his father. With his first real chance to get through to the older man, he made every word count. "For weeks, I've been trying to convince you there was someone after us and the Stuarts, but you wouldn't listen. Even when it was so obvious there was no other answer, you still wouldn't listen. But you're going to listen now, Dad. And when I'm finished, if you still intend to disown your only daughter because she had the courage to fall in love with Ian Stuart even though she knew what it would cost her—then you'd better get ready to disown me, too."

"What? You can't mean—"

"I've never meant anything more. I couldn't live

with myself if I turned my back on Michele just because she fell in love. And I sure as hell couldn't stay here and watch you pretend she didn't exist. There's been too much hate, and I'm tired of it. I don't give a damn what started the feud. All I know is that it's over. Ian and I won't fight."

"You'll fight," Charles said harshly. "When he hits, you'll hit back. And he will. It's in his blood. It's in your blood. Neither of you can escape it."

Jon heard a hollow laugh and realized it was his own—a sound of defeat; he didn't know what it would take to end his father's hate, but he doubted now that words would ever be enough. He leaned back against the desk and spoke quietly, without force or emotion.

"You want to talk about blood? Fine. Let's talk about that. Let's talk about the older half brother I probably have."

Charles stiffened, his face flushing suddenly with a new anger. "What are you talking about?"

Studying his father dispassionately, Jon said, "Yeah, I thought so. You knew. You knew Helen Gordon was pregnant when she left Atlanta."

"Pregnant with *his* bastard," Charles muttered, "not my child."

"His bastard—or your child? That's a fairly useless distinction considering that neither one of you married her. Did it ever occur to you in all these years to wonder whatever became of a son that *might* have been yours? Did you stop and think just once that the hate you and Brandon Stuart poured all over that poor woman might possibly come back to haunt you one day?"

For the first time, Charles couldn't meet his son's flat eyes. He was a little pale, clearly disturbed that Jon was quite obviously scornful of his behavior. A proud man, he had never received anything but respect from his son, and it shook him now to see and hear the contempt Jon didn't try to hide.

"You don't know how it was," he protested, attempting to work up the righteous anger that had never failed to accompany that bitter memory. Until now.

"I'm listening," Jon said evenly. "And you're going to tell me exactly how it was. Because we're out of time, Dad. What goes around comes around. Unless we find a way to stop him, there's a good chance we'll all be destroyed by a man who doesn't seem to give a tinker's damn which one of you is his father."

Michele was awakened by the phone for a second morning, and just as the day before, she again lay sleepily listening to the rumble of Ian's voice without really hearing the words. The last echoes of some kind of rhyme were fading in her mind, and though she felt an impulse to concentrate on it, the effort proved too much.

When her pillow moved, she murmured, " 'The Lady of Shalott,' " and frowned because that couldn't be right. She lifted her head and stared at Ian.

He was smiling a little, his eyes warm.

"It's a poem," she clarified.

"Tennyson," he agreed gravely. "What's the connection?"

She thought about that, but if there was a connection, it totally escaped her. "I wish," she said ruefully, "my subconscious would talk louder."

Ian raised his head and kissed her. "I love you," he murmured huskily.

"I love you, too." She smiled at him, but then her smile faded as the events of the day before surfaced in her mind. She felt a throb of loss inside her. "Was that . . . Jon on the phone?" she asked.

Nodding, Ian said quietly, "He sounded pretty exhausted. Apparently, he and your father were up most of the night."

"And?" She wasn't sure she wanted to hear.

"And—by the time Jon got through with him, he was quite a bit calmer about you and me. The subject of Helen Gordon seems to have taken most of the fight out of him, at least for now. I got the feeling Jon was pretty rough with him."

Michele wasn't surprised. "I always figured one day Jon would have to fight Dad about something important. What your father told you about strong-minded men breeding strong-minded sons is true, but Dad's never had to oppose that strength in Jon."

"He has now."

"I wonder what the result will be." Michele sighed. "And I wonder if Dad'll be able to accept us."

"He's at least accepted the fact that what happened thirty-five years ago has come back to haunt us all. Jon got the story out of him, but he thinks I should get Dad's side of it before we compare notes."

"I'll bet both sides are radically different," she mused wryly.

"No doubt of it. Anyway, I need to talk to Dad face to face and pry it out of him. He usually works in the office on Sunday, catching up on paperwork. I can see him there." He paused, then added, "Will you humor me and get some rest while I'm gone?"

Michele looked at the clock, and said, "I've been sleeping for nearly twelve hours."

Ian had obviously expected a protest. "I know,"

he said patiently, "but you've been under a hell of a strain, and one good night's sleep isn't going to ease that. I know you're worried; I am, too. But until we get all the facts, there's really nothing we can do about Nicholas Gordon."

Steadily, she said, "The message said today would be dangerous."

"Baby, every day is going to be dangerous until we stop this. I'll be careful. But I'd feel a lot better if I knew you were here watching a dumb movie on television or reading a book."

Michele was reluctant, but she saw the sense of what he was saying. Though he hadn't used the argument of her pregnancy, she knew he was concerned about that as well, and since she still felt tired despite the sleep, taking things easy was a good idea.

By the time Ian left the apartment a couple of hours later, she was ensconced on the couch with soft music playing and several books within reach. At first, it was peaceful, and she managed to concentrate on the novel she was reading. In fact, she became aware of her tension only when the phone rang and she jumped a foot in surprise.

"And it's not even a horror novel," she muttered to herself, picking up the receiver from the endtable. "Hello?"

"You sound annoyed," Ian noted.

"I am. The phone made me jump." She glanced at the clock, adding, "You've been gone an hour."

"Dad's being difficult," he explained. "He's talked a lot and hasn't said a damned thing. Now he wants to go over to the building and take another look at the damage. I didn't want you to worry if it took longer than I expected."

"Just be careful," she pleaded.

"I will."

After she'd hung up, Michele sat staring into space for several minutes, conscious of something nagging at her. No matter how hard she tried, she couldn't focus on it. It was like having a tune running through your head and *knowing* there were words to it lurking just out of reach.

Deciding that it wasn't going to come to her because she was trying too hard, she returned to her book and concentrated on absorbing those words. It was nearly half an hour before she got back into the story, and she jumped when the phone rang again.

"Hello?"

"Hi, Michele." Jon did sound tired, though a faint thread of amusement ran through his voice. "I just wanted you to know that your clothes are back in the closet."

The relief she felt was almost numbing. "Jon, what on earth did you say to him?"

"A lot. A hell of a lot, in fact. He isn't happy about it, Misha. That would be too much to hope for. The idea of Ian Stuart as his son-in-law makes him choke. But once I convinced him that being disowned wouldn't make a dent in your determination, he was pretty well forced to accept the idea." Gently, he added, "He loves you, you know."

Michele had a sneaking suspicion that it had been as much Jon's loyal support as anything else that had swayed her father, but she was too grateful at the results to care. "I never wanted to hurt him. I hope you told him that."

"I did."

"Thank you."

"Don't mention it." Jon sighed, then said restlessly, "As for the rest, it's not a pretty story. Has Ian gotten his father's version?"

"He's working on it now. At their building."

"I think I'll go over there. If Brandon Stuart's reluctant, maybe the shock of a Logan in his building will jar something loose."

Michele had to laugh. "Just be careful."

After she hung up for the second time, she caught herself brooding again. Even with her father's grudging acceptance of her relationship with Ian, she knew there were still likely to be storms from him; Charles Logan had hated too long to be able to put all his bitterness behind him, not overnight anyway, and not without a great deal of reluctance. Michele realized that, and she was prepared to face trouble when it came.

She wanted to hear the details of what had happened thirty-five years ago, but she thought she already knew enough to guess what had happened.

What occupied her mind now was the same nagging feeling of something overlooked, some vital piece of information that she had seen but not really taken notice of. She found herself on her feet, pacing the room, a tune in her mind she couldn't find the words for.

When the phone rang a third time, she answered almost absently. "Hello?"

"Michele, it's Jackie. Are you all right?"

"I'm fine."

"Your father—"

"He's calmed down. Jon talked to him. Did you just guess I'd be here at Ian's?"

"It made sense," Jackie said dryly. "Besides, I called your house this morning and Jon told me

where you were. He also said you'd gotten some kind
of warning that today wouldn't exactly be a good
day. Is Ian with you?"

The warning, Michele thought. That was it. Steve
had said he was going to express the original of that
enigmatic message, and he would have found a car-
rier that would deliver it even on a Sunday; the
guard at her office building would have it by now.
Something about that message had bothered her,
and she wanted to see the original.

"Michele?"

"What? Oh—no, he and Jon are both at the
Stuarts' building. There's something I have to do,
Jackie; can I call you later?"

"But, Michele, this warning—"

"I'll call you later. Bye, Jackie."

She took time only to jot a quick note for Ian on
the chance that he returned before she did, then
grabbed her purse and coat and hurriedly left the
apartment. She couldn't have said why it seemed so
important for her to see the message; she only knew
that the tune in her head was louder and more
emphatic.

Traffic was light, and her cab driver was more
than willing to wait while she went inside her office
building. The express delivery had been made, and
she carried the flat envelope back out to the taxi.

"Where to, ma'am?"

She gave him Ian's address automatically, occupied with opening the envelope. As she gazed at the
single sheet of un-lined paper in her lap, her first
realization was that Steve had taken no notice of the
*way* the message was written. Block-printing, he'd
said, and it was; but the sentences had been arranged with care and precision, one to each line,

with clear breaks after the first two and second two
lines.

She had copied the sentences as Steve had read
them aloud, never realizing that how the message
looked was even more important than what it said.
But some part of her mind had sensed a pattern
even so, and now she could see it clearly.

> *I must warn them*
> *Tell her this immediately.*
> *It is vital that she know*
> *Sunday is dangerous*
>
> *Story I told you was false*
> *Unable to tell you truth*
> *The buyer is no stranger*
> *Three devices, not one*
> *Only they can stop him*
> *Next days critical*

For a long, cold moment, what she saw made no
sense. But then everything came together in her
mind. She knew what had nagged at her, knew why
she had awakened this morning with the title of a
poem on her lips; her subconscious had been prod-
ding her, because it had been there all along. The
answer.

Unsteadily, she told the driver she'd changed
her mind, and gave him the address of the Stuarts'
building. While he uncomplainingly changed direc-
tion, she stared down at the warning in her lap.
Now that she saw it, the hidden warning stood out
clearly. The first letter of each line spelled out a
simple message: IT IS SUTTON.

*    *    *

There were no men downstairs in the lobby. No evidence of security. Michele knew that wasn't right, Ian wouldn't have reduced security. She hurried across the lobby, sparing only a glance for the single elevator standing open; it would have been quicker, but she took the stairs.

The tenth floor. Ian had said the damage was on the tenth floor, so that's where they'd be. It took an eternity to climb the stairs, and with every step her fear grew. He couldn't have gotten here already, surely? Not from Jackie's. But perhaps he hadn't been with her, perhaps he'd only called her and said something casual like, "Find out from Michele where Ian and Jon are, I'd like to talk to them about better security."

And Jackie, poor Jackie, wouldn't have thought twice about the request. She'd been Cole's pipeline for months, feeding him information without ever realizing that was what he was after, more than willing to talk about the bitter hatred of the feud because she'd been raised on all the stories. She'd told him about Ian and Michele, their meeting on Martinique. Michele knew now why Jackie's attitude had changed so suddenly on the island; because she had called her lover, and Cole had convinced her that her friend needed someone on her side. The last thing he'd wanted was a rift between the two women—even with the chance of a dangerously strong tie forming between Michele and Ian.

Michele reached the tenth floor at last and, breathless, pushed open the heavy fire door.

They were all there. Ian, Jon, and Brandon Stuart were standing in a loose group just a few feet away across from the elevators. Before Michele could realize they weren't alone, a strong hand grabbed her arm and flung her into the group.

Ian caught her before she could fall, and pulled her into the shelter of his arm so that she was standing between him and Jon. And even though she would have chosen to be with him no matter what happened, the anguish in his eyes as he drew her close to his side made her heart ache.

"It's a pity everyone isn't here," Cole said conversationally. He was holding a wicked black automatic in one hand, and it was obvious he knew how to handle guns. He looked at Michele, and the easy, charming smile quirked his lips. "Didn't happen to bring Pop along, did you?"

Michele thought she had never seen anything as empty as his eyes. His gray eyes, she realized. He must have worn tinted contact lenses until now. *A strange, but familiar face, eyes veiled against you.* It made so much sense now.

"So you've guessed Charles Logan is your father?" Jon asked in an even tone.

Cole laughed, his empty eyes flicking to Michele again. "Once I saw her, it was fairly obvious. I look more like her brother than you do. Not that it matters, really. I don't care which side of the feud spawned me."

"Then why destroy us?" Brandon asked quietly.

"You destroyed my mother," Cole told him in the same eerily conversational tone. "Both of you. When she found out she was pregnant, you threw her out, because you thought I wasn't yours. And Logan wasn't about to take her back after that, even though she loved him, too. He didn't give a damn whose kid she was carrying. She told me. She told me how both of you called her those ugly names."

Cole's expressionless face quivered for an instant, raw hatred flashing hotly in his eyes. The emotion was like the dank air of a tomb; something shut up in darkness and silence for too long. "And she told me—*I* should have had a real name instead of one she had to make up. She told me we'd get even one day. She found a book about the feud, and we read it together. We made plans. It was poetic justice that the feud should destroy you both."

"But it won't," Michele said softly. "You're going to do that."

"That's your fault," Cole snapped. "It would have worked perfectly if only you'd believed what you should have. I thought you understood the feud." He nodded toward Ian. "You should have hated him when I made it look like he'd hurt your brother. Why didn't you hate him?" It was almost a plea.

Michele felt so cold she could hardly keep her teeth from chattering. He was insane, lost somewhere totally beyond their reach.

"Why?" Cole repeated the question, though this time it was in a voice crackling with hostility.

She held her voice steady with an effort. "Because I love him."

Abruptly calm again, Cole said chidingly, "That was a stupid mistake. Now you'll have to die with him." He stepped back, carefully moving around the roped-off area in front of the ruined elevators. "I have this last elevator all ready for you. I'll send the car to the top of the building, and then the charges I've set there will snap the cable." Holding the gun trained steadily on them, he pressed the button to summon the functional express car.

"You won't get away with this," Brandon told him harshly.

"Oh, I think I will," Cole replied with a smile. "This time, I've planted careful evidence. Everyone will believe that Charles Logan is responsible. I've thought it out, and I think that's best. I'll be able to watch him suffer while people say he killed his children as well as his enemies. One day, if I think he's suffered enough, I'll kill him, too."

From the corner of her eye, Michele saw Ian and Jon exchange quick glances, and she knew that neither of them would walk meekly into the elevator. Ian's arm tightened around her, and she realized he was getting ready to push her aside in the instant before he leaped toward Cole.

She was frozen, unable to move or make a sound.

The prosaic ding of the arriving elevator car didn't distract Cole's attention from them, but as the doors opened a furious voice succeeded all too well.

"What the hell is this all about?" Charles Logan demanded wrathfully, stepping out of the car. His fierce gray eyes swept the paralyzed group a few feet in front of him, almost jerking away when they encountered the sight of his daughter in the shelter of Ian Stuart's embrace.

He saw Cole then, and in the eternal moment that they looked at each other face to face for the first time, it was obvious that Charles Logan recognized this man as his son. The expression in his eyes was pain and regret—and acceptance.

For a long time afterward, Michele wondered if, in the end, that was the one thing Cole was unable to bear. Because if there was any sanity left in him, it must have been the most bitter blow of all that after the long years of hatred, he looked into his father's eyes for the first time—and knew without a doubt that he could have claimed his birthright.

Cole let out a hoarse cry and stumbled back, the

hand not holding the gun lifting as if to ward off some horror. Maybe he forgot about the gaping elevator doors his own handiwork had left jammed open. Or maybe he just lost his balance.

Ian and Jon tried to reach him, but they were too late.

It took hours to explain what was necessary to the police, hours of questions and statements. A past buried for too long had to be exhumed and minutely examined even as Cole's body was extricated from the bottom of the elevator shaft and carried away in a coroner's wagon and a bomb was safely defused. The security men, told to leave the building by Brandon Stuart after Cole had forced him to give the order, returned, a bit sheepish that they hadn't realized the order was made under duress.

The police were, to put it mildly, upset to find that sabotage had gone on for several weeks without being reported, and they had a number of harsh things to say about the matter. But the Logan/Stuart feud was as real—if incomprehensible—to them as it was to the principals, and so they were less severe than they might have been.

Or their almost unwilling compassion might have sprung from a different source. The feud had caused a death for the first time in more than a century, and though the result of that was never alluded to, it was obvious that the haunting final battle had ended that war forever.

Michele knew that. She sat close beside Ian in the lounge where the police had taken their statements, and though it hurt her to see her father's face she couldn't stop looking at him. As the entire sordid story had been pieced together in this quiet room, she had watched those fierce eyes lose their fire and that strong face slacken and go gray. It had taken a series of near-tragedies and one final one to bring home to Charles Logan the devastation of hate, and it wasn't a lesson he could ignore.

He had fathered a child thirty-five years ago, but his worst sin hadn't been disclaiming that fact; he was just as responsible for the seeds of hate as those of life.

The feud was over, but the cost had been terrible. There was no way of knowing what Cole might have been, and though Michele couldn't grieve for the man who had fallen to his death, she was saddened by the waste of his life.

And then there was Jackie.

"Somebody has to tell her," Michele said to Jon when the police finally began putting away their notebooks.

Her brother looked at her for a long moment, then said simply, "I don't know if I can."

Michele understood his reluctance. Of them all, Jackie had been the innocent pawn, ruthlessly used and sacrificed. She had been taught to hate, her mind filled with tales of treachery and worse, then she had lost her heart to a man who had set out to seduce her for his own mad purpose.

Jon knew only too well how Jackie would feel when she discovered the truth about Cole. And he knew there was every chance she would never forgive him for his part in what had happened to her; if she had never been taught to hate, she might never have been a tool for Cole to use.

"I don't know if I can," Jon repeated.

"You have to," Michele told him gently.

He knew that, too. "Yes. I'll . . . take Dad home and then go to her."

Brandon Stuart, who had been listening to them in silence, said to Jon, "You go ahead. I'll take Charles home. He shouldn't be alone."

The shocks of the day had had a numbing effect, and Michele felt only faint surprise as she looked at Ian's father. "You?"

He smiled just a little. "Why not? We're going to have to make peace or risk losing our children—and grandchildren. We might as well start now." He rose and went over to Charles Logan, who watched his approach with grim eyes.

Michele almost held her breath; she could feel both Ian and Jon waiting with just as much tension. And it was somehow ironic that the first words spoken by the two old warriors directly to each other in more than three decades were both prosaic and completely in character.

"If you came in the Mercedes," Brandon Stuart said, "you can drive us."

Charles Logan got slowly to his feet, still frowning. Irritably, he said, "I'll be damned if I will. My car's never had a Stuart in it."

"There is," Brandon said, "a first time for everything. Come on, I'll buy you a cup of coffee."

"I'll buy my own," Charles muttered, but he was moving with the other man toward the hallway.

The two policemen still in the room stared after them as if they couldn't quite believe their eyes.

Hours later, curled up beside Ian on his couch, Michele was still finding it hard to believe. "Just . . . walked out together," she murmured. "Two nice men going for coffee."

Proving that he understood what shock could do to people, Ian mused, "Think they'll still be speaking to each other at our wedding?"

"They're both numb, I think. That's bound to wear off eventually. But . . . after today, I can believe in almost anything."

They hadn't talked much about Cole, not because either had forgotten the final sight—and sound—of him, but because it was still too much with them to be discussed. Michele had explained her sudden arrival at the building, showing Ian the original of the warning and telling him about the other realizations she'd had. First had been her nagging awareness that it was unlikely their enemy could have known she had gotten involved with Ian on Martinique; so busy stirring things up in Atlanta, how could he have known? Unless, she had realized, he was in touch with the only "friend" on the island—Jackie.

The "Lady of Shalott" her subconscious had prodded her with that morning had been perfectly clear once she had made the proper connection. It hadn't been the poem itself, but a few words of a single line that had floated around in her mind.

"Which words?" Ian had asked.

" 'The mirror cracked.' I must have been thinking of a reflection that wasn't quite right. I'd thought before that Cole looked familiar, but I didn't know who he reminded me of."

"I knew when he popped out of nowhere waving that gun," Ian had admitted. "But at the party Friday night, all I knew was that something bothered me about the four of you standing together."

Michele didn't like to think about the frightening moments before Cole's death, but she couldn't help but wonder about her father's timely arrival.

"Did you hear what Dad told the police about why he'd come to the building?"

"He said he'd gotten a call warning him that you and Jon were in danger," Ian remembered.

After a thoughtful moment, Michele said, "We've had a lot of helpful warnings, haven't we? Almost as if somebody was watching over us."

"Like you said, after today, I'd be willing to believe in almost anything. All I know for sure is that I love you, Michele Logan."

Glorying in the one certainty that had never wavered despite the odds against it, she murmured, "I love you, too, Ian Stuart." And gave herself up to the wonder of that.

# Epilogue

Snow fell on Christmas Eve. It wasn't totally un-
heard of in the Deep South, but it was certainly
unusual enough to merit considerable comment. And
though Northerners innured to harsh winters would
have considered the scant few inches of white stuff
no more than a minor inconvenience, snowplows
were rare birds in Atlanta, and the city had come to
a virtual standstill.

Michele loved it.

She thought it was apt that after meeting Ian
on a hot island paradise and then struggling with
him to preserve their love through weeks of cold
rain and sleet, they should be married while an
uncommon snowfall blanketed the ground outside
the tiny church they had chosen. Apt and curiously
symbolic of the starkly different stages of their relationship: the tropical heat of passion, the cold rain
of worry and anguish, the soft snowfall of peace and
contentment.

Michele felt that peace, and it grew even stronger to merge with an almost overwhelming wave of love as Ian slipped his arms around her from behind and rested his chin on top of her head.

"You're very quiet, wife," he murmured.

She smiled, still gazing out the window of their bedroom at the falling snow. "I was just thinking how confused some of the newspapers seemed to be. They didn't know whether to headline the first Christmas Eve snow in ages, or the first wedding ever between a Logan and a Stuart."

The last couple of weeks had been decidedly hectic, not the least because Charles Logan's (reluctant but resigned) announcement of his daughter's engagement to Ian Stuart had created more than a nine-days' wonder.

Ian had gotten impatient at one point after being badgered by a newsman, and had demanded to know if there weren't more important stories going on in the world. With a somewhat comical frankness, the journalist replied that the world was pretty quiet just now and, besides—five hundred years!

Remembering that day, Ian chuckled. "We may have lost part of the headlines today, but I caught a glimpse of that pesky reporter peering into the church, and he had his notebook. And since even a blind man could have seen how much resolution it took for your father to give you to me, I'll bet our fifteen minutes of fame aren't up yet."

Michele couldn't help but laugh, grateful that they could at last find humor in the final remnants of the feud. "I was about ready to turn around and glare at him when he finally sputtered the right answer. Jon told me later that he poked Dad in the ribs just to make sure he got his line right."

Sobering a bit, Ian asked, "What about him and Jackie? I was surprised to see her in the church."

"She's still pretty shattered, and Jon's sticking close. If she comes out of this without blaming him . . . then maybe they have a chance together. It'll take time, though." Turning in his arms, she lifted hers around his neck, smiling up at him. "And maybe . . . a little good fortune."

Ian, who knew by now about the odd dream Michele had experienced while waiting for him to come home, gazed down on her lovely face and admitted silently that sometimes fortune was so astonishingly good that it *had* to be a little magic. Aloud, he said only, "The hand of destiny?"

"A roll of the dice, a turn of the card, a fork in the road. Maybe it was fate that my car stalled that day. Or fortune."

"Or fortune," Ian agreed, bending his head to kiss her.

In a lamplit study a considerable number of miles north of Atlanta, an old man with a full white beard and wise dark eyes sat at a massive desk. He put a file folder aside, his benign face smiling, then drew another from the stack near the blotter.

He opened the file and studied the contents, nodding to himself from time to time. A difficult case, he mused silently, his elegant hands sifting through the papers. But not impossible, of course.

Nothing was impossible.

If you enjoyed **STAR-CROSSED LOVERS**, be sure to look for Kay Hooper's unforgettable historical romance from FANFARE, **THE MATCH-MAKER,** on sale in September 1991.

In **THE MATCHMAKER,** a novel of sheer magic set at the turn of the century, Kay Hooper tells the simply thrilling tale of Cyrus Fortune, the mysterious figure who has guided the destinies of many lovers. Cyrus, who has always been known as a womanizer, has fallen passionately in love with Julia Drummond. Julia is unhappily married—but promises never to break her vows. In the following excerpt Cyrus follows Julia to the library where they speak for the first time.

"Hello."
Julia stiffened, recognizing the voice even though she'd never heard it, because it matched the nakedly sensual warmth of black eyes. Slowly, she turned her head, recapturing her aloof mask with the ease of long and constant practice. She watched him stroll across the room, the size and lazy grace of him making her feel a panicky, threatened sensation. He sat down in the chair on the other side of the table and looked at her with that bold stare, and she felt suddenly exposed. Vulnerable.
With all the coldness she could muster, she said, "I don't believe we've been introduced."
His well—shaped mouth curved in a smile. "No, but then, we know who we are, don't we? I'm Cyrus Fortune, and you're Julia Drummond." The words were terse to the point of rudeness, his manner was definitely arrogant—but the voice was elegant black velvet.
Julia began to understand Anne's warning about the need for a chastity belt. She would have sworn she was the last woman in Richmond who could have felt any temptation to break her marriage vows, but that voice affected her like nothing ever had. In her mind was a strangely vivid little image of the way a cat arched its back when it was stroked, in an instinctive ripple of unthinking

pleasure, and she wondered dimly if the sound of her racing heart was anything like a purr.

"I've been watching you tonight," he said. "But you know that. Do you know I've been watching you for days?"

That was a shock, but one she endured silently. She had to stop this before . . . before it was too late. Her own thoughts were scattered, panicked, and she didn't even know why or how he could affect her like this. She drew a deep breath; it felt as if she hadn't breathed at all until then. "Mr. Fortune—"

"Cyrus." It was less a request than a command.

Julia ignored it. "Mr. Fortune, I'm a married woman—"

"Drummond must have robbed the cradle to get you," Fortune said abruptly, cutting her off without civility. "Somebody said you'd been married for two years, but you can't be a day over eighteen."

Oddly enough, Julia knew she couldn't accuse him of trying to flatter her; she had a strong conviction that Fortune was too blunt a man to waste time with insincere compliments—even to get a woman into his bed. He wouldn't need to resort to such tricks, she admitted to herself silently, and was appalled at the realization.

Holding her voice even, she said, "I'm twenty-one, Mr. Fortune. And I am *very* married."

His mouth quirked again in that mocking little smile. "Not tempted to stray? Drummond can't be such a good lover; the man's heavy-handed with his horses."

The sheer effrontery of that remark made Julia gasp. Her own nature was toward frankness—or it had been, before her marriage—and she was hardly a prude, but for any man to speak to a woman in such a way went beyond the bounds of good taste *and* decency. But before she could gather her wits, he was going on, and if she'd thought he had gone as far as possible already, she was in for another shock.

"Drummond isn't making you happy and we both know it, Julia. You're frozen inside; I can see it. You were never meant to be that way. Red hair is a badge of passion, and yours is like fire. I've never seen hair so red or eyes so wildly green. Or such an erotic mouth, like a lush flower. You have a magnificent body, a body made for pleasure. Even those dull colors and fabrics you wear can't hide your wonderful form. And you move with such grace, as if you hear music."

"Don't—" she got out in a strangled gasp, but he went on in his black velvet voice that made even the reprehensible words a sensual caress.

"Drummond wouldn't know what to do with a woman like you. I'm sure of it. He can't appreciate the fire in you. He probably takes you in the dark with your nightgown pulled up and thinks of nothing but his own pleasure. Does he apologize when he turns to you with his carnal appetites, Julia? Does he make it a hurried, shameful act instead of something joyful?" Fortune uttered a low laugh that was derisive. "Gentlemen like Drummond believe there are only two kinds of women: ladies and whores—and only whores enjoy bedding men. So the gentlemen marry ladies and fumble in the dark to breed. Is that all you want? To be a broodmare and never feel the hot pleasure of real passion?"

He laughed again, his eyes blacker than anything she'd ever seen and filled with a heat that burned her. "I'm no gentleman, Julia. I dont want a lady or a whore in my bed—just a woman. A beautiful woman. I won't apologize for wanting her and I'll look at her naked in the light because God meant for a woman to be seen by a man. And touched by a man."

She wasn't conscious of moving until she was halfway across the room, her heart thudding, the smothering sensation of panic overwhelming her. She didn't go to the door that led back to the ballroom but another one, and she had no idea where it would take her. It didn't matter. Anywhere. Anywhere as long as she could escape him.

"Julia."

That voice. It tugged at her—and the realization she could scarcely resist terrified her. Her hand on the door handle, she half turned to stare at him. He had risen to his feet, but didn't move toward her. He was smiling almost gently.

"I want you. I want you in my bed."

"No." It didn't come from morals or consciousness of her marriage vows, or anything else of which society would have approved. It didn't come from a lack of attraction, shocking though that was to her; she felt the attraction, the strange, irresistible pulling at all her senses. The denial came from deep inside her, without thought, spurred by instinct.

"I can make you happy," he said.

"You can destroy me," she heard herself whisper.

"One of the most versatile and talented authors of the last decade." -- *Romantic Times*

Enter the irresistible world of

# *Amanda Quick*

Bestselling romance writer Amanda Quick takes us back to the days of Regency England in these stirring novels of love and adventure.

☐ *Seduction*     28354-5     $4.50

☐ *Surrender*     28594-7     $4.50

☐ *Scandal*     28932-2     $4.95

Available wherever Bantam Fanfare Books are sold or use this page for ordering:

# THE LATEST IN BOOKS
# AND AUDIO CASSETTES

## Paperbacks

| | | | |
|---|---|---|---|
| ☐ | 28671 | **NOBODY'S FAULT** Nancy Holmes | $5.95 |
| ☐ | 28412 | **A SEASON OF SWANS** Celeste De Blasis | $5.95 |
| ☐ | 28354 | **SEDUCTION** Amanda Quick | $4.50 |
| ☐ | 28594 | **SURRENDER** Amanda Quick | $4.50 |
| ☐ | 28435 | **WORLD OF DIFFERENCE** Leonia Blair | $5.95 |
| ☐ | 28416 | **RIGHTFULLY MINE** Doris Mortman | $5.95 |
| ☐ | 27032 | **FIRST BORN** Doris Mortman | $4.95 |
| ☐ | 27283 | **BRAZEN VIRTUE** Nora Roberts | $4.50 |
| ☐ | 27891 | **PEOPLE LIKE US** Dominick Dunne | $4.95 |
| ☐ | 27260 | **WILD SWAN** Celeste De Blasis | $5.95 |
| ☐ | 25692 | **SWAN'S CHANCE** Celeste De Blasis | $5.95 |
| ☐ | 27790 | **A WOMAN OF SUBSTANCE** Barbara Taylor Bradford | $5.95 |

## Audio

☐ **SEPTEMBER** by Rosamunde Pilcher
Performance by Lynn Redgrave
180 Mins. Double Cassette     45241-X    $15.95

☐ **THE SHELL SEEKERS** by Rosamunde Pilcher
Performance by Lynn Redgrave
180 Mins. Double Cassette     48183-9    $14.95

☐ **COLD SASSY TREE** by Olive Ann Burns
Performance by Richard Thomas
180 Mins. Double Cassette     45166-9    $14.95

☐ **NOBODY'S FAULT** by Nancy Holmes
Performance by Geraldine James
180 Mins. Double Cassette     45250-9    $14.95

---